"Com

Nick said, certain there were worse ways to wake up with amnesia. Emily jumped visibly. "I just want a kiss," he chided gently. "I didn't ask you to make love to me."

The pink in her cheeks deepened. "I know, I just thought…" She shrugged and stepped closer. "Nick," she protested as he drew her down onto the hospital bed, "I really don't think this is the…ah…place."

Nick. He could get used to being called Nick, especially with that breathless way Emily had of talking. Lifting his arm, he traced the delicate lines of her face. Her skin was like the finest silk. Her lips were moist and velvety. And she had a faintly stubborn line to her jaw, which contrasted adorably with her angelic sweetness.

Nick couldn't remember being in love with his wife…but he'd immediately fallen into lust!

Dear Reader,

What a special lineup of love stories Silhouette Romance has for you this month. Bestselling author Sandra Steffen continues her BACHELOR GULCH miniseries with *Clayton's Made-Over Mrs.* And in *The Lawman's Legacy*, favorite author Phyllis Halldorson introduces a special promotion called MEN! Who says good men are hard to find?! Plus, we've got Julianna Morris's *Daddy Woke up Married*—our BUNDLES OF JOY selection—*Love, Marriage and Family 101* by Anne Peters, *The Scandalous Return of Jake Walker* by Myrna Mackenzie and *The Cowboy Who Broke the Mold* by Cathleen Galitz, who makes her Silhouette debut as one of our WOMEN TO WATCH.

I hope you enjoy all six of these wonderful novels. In fact, I'd love to get your thoughts on Silhouette Romance. If you'd like to share your comments about the Silhouette Romance line, please send a letter directly to my attention: Melissa Senate, Senior Editor, Silhouette Books, 300 E. 42nd St., 6th Floor, New York, NY 10017. I welcome all of your comments, and here are a few particulars I'd like to have your feedback on:
1) Why do you enjoy Silhouette Romance?
2) What types of stories would you like to see more of? Less of?
3) Do you have favorite authors?

Your thoughts about Romance are very important to me. After all, these books are for you! Again, I hope you enjoy our six novels this month—and that you'll write me with your thoughts.

Regards,

Melissa Senate
Senior Editor
Silhouette Books

Please address questions and book requests to:
Silhouette Reader Service
U.S.: 3010 Walden Ave., P.O. Box 1325, Buffalo, NY 14269
Canadian: P.O. Box 609, Fort Erie, Ont. L2A 5X3

DADDY WOKE
UP MARRIED

Julianna Morris

Silhouette
R O M A N C E™
Published by Silhouette Books
America's Publisher of Contemporary Romance

To Carol Duncan, for all your support and advice.
To Micki and Peg, for your words of encouragement when
I really needed them. And a special thanks to Cathleen,
for your enthusiasm and help as an editor.

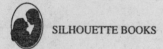 SILHOUETTE BOOKS

ISBN 0-373-19252-5

DADDY WOKE UP MARRIED

Copyright © 1997 by Martha Ann Ford

Printed in U.S.A.

Books by Julianna Morris

Silhouette Romance

Baby Talk #1097
Family of Three #1178
Daddy Woke up Married #1252

JULIANNA MORRIS

has an offbeat sense of humor, which frequently gets her into trouble. She is often accused of being curious about everything...her interests ranging from oceanography and photography to traveling, antiquing, walking on the beach and reading science fiction. Choosing a college major was extremely difficult, but after many changes she earned a bachelor's degree in environmental science.

Julianna's writing is supervised by a cat named Gandalf, who sits on the computer monitor and criticizes each keystroke. Ultimately, she would like a home overlooking the ocean, where she can write to her heart's content—and Gandalf's malcontent. She'd like to share that home with her own romantic hero, someone with a warm, sexy smile, lots of patience and an offbeat sense of humor to match her own. Oh, yes...and he has to like cats.

Dear Reader,

A recent acquaintance of mine freezes when babies are mentioned. He literally seems paralyzed by the thought of an unpredictable little human who can scream and make a dirty diaper at the same time. Poor guy, he doesn't know what he's missing.

These unpredictable little humans are precious gifts. Each one is different, and unique, and a miracle in his or her own right. They will walk into the future with the lessons of life and love imparted by parents, teachers, friends and even strangers. They are frightening and wonderful.

And babies are fun! They laugh and play with their toes. They fingerpaint with strained peas and carrots. Each day they grow a little more, expanding their world, and getting into mischief. I remember countless times my nephews and nieces did something "naughty," and I'd be laughing so hard, I couldn't scold them.

Someday when I hold my own bundle of joy, I know I'll be overwhelmed, terrified and deliriously happy. They are a huge responsibility, and a remarkable privilege— truly creations of the heart. As for the dirty diapers? They're a small price to pay.

Best wishes…

Julianna Morris

Chapter One

"Is it safe up there?"

"Define *safe*."

Emily put her hands on her hips and glared at the man perched on her roof. He looked like an actor in a Coke commercial—faded jeans, no shirt, and sweat gleaming on his pectoral muscles. Not to mention brown hair, brown eyes and a smile that had cut swaths through feminine hearts from Seattle to Singapore. If she hadn't grown up with Nick Carleton treating her like his baby sister, she might have thought he was sexy. Instead, she mostly thought he was aggravating.

"That isn't funny. You know exactly what I mean."

Nick grinned to himself. He could always count on Emily to get huffy when he teased her. She was a nice kid, though she drove him crazy half the time—it only seemed fair to do the same to her. "Guilty conscience? As I recall, you ordered me to fix your leaky roof. And me on vacation, no less."

"Would you prefer me to fix it myself?" she asked

sweetly. She shooed her cat, GeeZee, away from the ladder and put her foot on the bottom rung. "I'll come up now."

Damn. He scowled into her mischievous blue eyes. "You get on that ladder and I'll paddle your bottom."

"I'm *so-o-o* scared."

"Brat," Nick muttered.

"I heard that." Emily stepped back and grinned. Nick was a dear, even if he had the mentality of a Neanderthal. When he'd learned the details of her first marriage, he'd wanted to rip Kevin's heart out and stuff it down his throat. Emily had been tempted to let him. The muscles in her jaw tightened for an instant as she thought about Kevin.

"Hey, kid. Something wrong?"

Emily relaxed at the gentle tone in Nick's voice, then shook her head. Kevin wasn't a part of her life anymore; she didn't have to think about him. "I'm fine."

"Sure? You aren't…er…yourself right now."

Her nose wrinkled. "You worry too much." She patted her rounded stomach. She hadn't begun wearing real maternity clothes around the house—relying on roomy summer knits—but her pregnancy was unquestionably showing. "I'm only going to have a baby."

"I remember. *Perfectly,*" Nick said distinctly.

She smothered a laugh at his red-faced expression. Nick's reaction had been typically male when she'd confided her desire for a baby, and her decision to have one through the medical alternative to sex. He'd stomped out of the house with his sense of propriety offended. Several hours later he'd returned with an outrageous proposal…he'd donate the sperm, and in return would get to play a role in his child's life. But he'd had one condition—they had to get married, at least until after the baby arrived.

At first she'd thought it was a ridiculous idea. But after a lengthy argument, it began to make sense. Nick was a perennial bachelor, with a job that took him out of the country on a regular basis. He'd probably never get married and have children. This way he could be a father without having to face any of those things, which as a man, he was naturally averse to...commitment and dirty diapers.

A platonic marriage—with separate residences—fit Nick's overly protective attitude toward her and seemed perfect for them both.

Even so, Emily knew he'd found his participation in the artificial insemination procedure terribly embarrassing, and she was grateful she'd succeeded in getting pregnant on their *first* trip to the doctor's office.

"Don't think about it," she advised him. "Besides, you were the one who insisted on being the father."

"That's not the point. Say, did you know that if you lean way over like this, you can see the harbor from here?"

Emily rolled her eyes at the blatant change of subject. "I can see Crockett Harbor from the front, why do I care about the back?" She added in a muttered undertone, "Chicken."

"I heard that."

"Fine. If the feathers fit...?"

"You—"

Nick's protest ended abruptly as his foot skidded against a loose piece of roofing material. Unbalanced by leaning "way over like this," he tumbled over the edge.

Everything seemed to happen in slow motion. The ladder tottered and crashed, a shower of shingles flew across the yard in a frenzied arc, and GeeZee gave out a screeching howl before flying under the hydrangea bush.

Emily didn't scream...not quite. But she gasped and rushed to where Nick lay tangled with the ladder.

"Nick?"

Nothing, not even a groan. But the single drop of blood trickling down his forehead convinced her this wasn't one of his usual gags.

"Lord," she muttered and raced into the house. She grabbed the phone and dialed for emergency services. "Hello?" she said breathlessly into the receiver. "My...er...husband just fell off the roof." It felt strange saying Nick was her husband, but much easier than going into a lengthy explanation—that they were only married on paper.

The dispatcher responded with soothing efficiency, eliciting facts in a clear, concise fashion. She promised a rescue unit would be sent immediately.

With a muttered "thank you" Emily dropped the receiver and hurried outside. Nick blinked and groaned, and Emily sagged with relief. It was small comfort to be sure, but at least he was alive—breathing was always better than *not* breathing.

"Nick...can you hear me? Are you all right?" she asked.

He mumbled something indiscernible.

The wail of sirens reassured her, though she could tell from the pained expression in his confused brown eyes that he didn't appreciate the noise. The sirens stopped in front of the house, and a minute later three men in emergency uniforms hurried through the gate by the garage, followed closely by a couple of Crockett, Washington, police officers and several firemen.

"You'll be all right," Emily whispered. She lightly touched Nick's hand. It was all her fault, she shouldn't have distracted him while he was working. At least he'd fallen from the one-story roof of the porch, rather than the second level of the old house.

"Excuse me, ma'am," one of the rescue workers murmured. He patted Emily's shoulder and took her place at Nick's side. "Let's take a look here."

"He fell," she explained quite unnecessarily—since there wasn't any other explanation for the ladder, scattered shingles and Nick's obvious injuries. "He was knocked out for a minute."

Without actually ignoring her, they checked Nick's vital signs, tried to get a coherent answer, strapped him into a neck brace and backboard, and lifted him onto the stretcher. Between the bandages and brace he looked awful.

Emily followed them to the ambulance, her hands trembling with alarm. "Sh...should I take my own car?"

Their gaze settled on the unmistakable swell of her stomach. "Er...no, ma'am. You're pretty shaken up. You'd better ride with your husband."

"Husband?" Nick muttered. "Whose husband? Cripes, my head hurts."

"Take it easy, mister. Your wife is right here," the leader of the rescue team assured.

Emily chafed impatiently when they insisted on taking her blood pressure and pulse before starting for the hospital. "I'm fine," she said. "Let's go." As the sirens wailed again she dropped her head back and took several long, deep, calming breaths. So much for a quiet summer weekend.

* * *

Ouch.

His first truly coherent thought was that every molecule in his body hurt. And the rocking and jolting beneath him didn't help a bit.

After a while most of the rocking stopped and a pencil-thin beam of light stabbed into his eyes. "Damn," he said aloud.

"Good, he's conscious. Nick? Do you understand what I'm saying?"

Nick? Who the hell was Nick, he wondered. Was it him? Somewhere in his pain-fogged head he remembered seeing a blue-eyed angel who was supposed to be his wife, but the details seemed too much to grasp. Angels didn't get married, they sat on clouds playing harps. So maybe that meant he was dead.

"Nick," the voice repeated, "do you understand what I'm saying?"

"Yeah," he muttered, hoping they'd just be quiet.

"Good. We're taking you in for some X rays," the voice informed him. "I don't think anything is broken, but I want to be sure."

Hell.

They weren't going to leave him alone. But apparently he wasn't dead, though it might be a pleasant alternative to his present state. He endured another bit of jolting, then some idiot told him to hold still. Very funny. He wasn't a masochist. He didn't have any intention of moving...not for about a million years.

The lights flashing overhead hurt his eyes, so he closed them tightly. A warm fog slid around him, soothing the pain, blocking out the demanding voices and pushy hands. He wished the angel was back. Her voice had been soft and melodic. Much nicer than these sadists.

After a while he grew annoyed with the poking and prodding and quietly insistent demands from unfamiliar voices. But when he finally pried his eyes open he found the pain had settled to a dull throb.

A door opened in the background, then a white-coated woman leaned over him.

"Where am I?" he asked, his throat raspy.

"In the hospital. You should learn not to jump off the roof—it's too hard on the body. You're not exactly Superman, you know."

"Very funny." He glared at the doctor, who obviously had learned her bedside manner from the Marx brothers. "Who are you?"

"Hmm…I'm Dr. Wescott. You don't recognize me?"

A vague alarm clamored through him. "Uh, well, not really. Should I?"

The attractive redhead tapped her fingers on her stethoscope. "Can you tell me your name?" she asked, instead of answering his question.

"Sure, I'm…" The room spun lazily while he fought a growing panic. "I'm…"

Nick.

Husband.

Wife.

They were just words out of the fog, with nothing solid to attach them to. "Uh…my wife, where's my wife?" He stalled, fighting the mad rush of his heart. Surely he would remember in a minute. He'd remember his identity…his *wife.*

"You mean Emily?"

"Yeah…Emily." He grasped at the name, though it

didn't seem any more familiar than *Nick* had sounded. "Where's Emily?"

"Waiting outside. She's been pretty worried about you."

For some reason that comforted him. Things couldn't be so bad if the angel was waiting, worried about him. Maybe when he saw her, he'd remember everything.

The doctor put down the side railing of the bed, then lifted his arm and touched the pulse point at his wrist. "We admitted you three hours ago, but you only completely lost consciousness for a couple of minutes right after the accident. That's good. You're going to be fine, aside from a few bruises and a mild concussion. I'll order more tests, but nothing is broken," she explained.

Nothing but my memory.

"Can you tell me your name?" she asked again.

He sighed. "I think it's Nick."

"Good. Now what else do you remember?"

"I don't even remember *that,*" he said dismally. "But I heard someone call me Nick."

"That's a start. Your name is Nick…Nicholas Carleton. Now, you asked about your wife…?"

His head throbbed worse as he pieced together the brief memories scattered in his brain. "I woke up and a woman was there—some guy said she was my wife. That's all I know. But hell, at least I've got a family. That's something to be grateful for, right?" Damn. He hated the edge in his voice, the need for reassurance.

"Yes." The physician nodded. "Okay, let's try some easy stuff. Do you know who's president?"

He looked at her in disbelief. "President? I may have amnesia, but even *I* know that's a little corny," he said before answering.

The woman laughed. "I see your personality is intact.

We'll try something else. Do you know what planet you're on?''

He snorted. ''Unless I've been abducted by extremely clever aliens, I'm on earth.'' Before she could ask anything else, he volunteered a series of impersonal facts. It was strange to realize he could remember who was president of the United States, and the number of innings in a standard baseball game, but couldn't recall the most basic details of his life.

Dr. Wescott fiddled for another couple of minutes, checking his eyesight and reflexes and asking questions before giving him a reassuring smile. ''You have amnesia, Nick. But don't worry, I'm sure it's only temporary. It's not unusual to have some memory loss after a blow to the head.''

Temporary amnesia? He swallowed. Yeah, that sounded possible. He hoped. ''Is Emily...can I see her now?''

She patted his shoulder. ''Of course, it'll just be a minute. I need to explain what's happened.'' She walked to the door, and he caught a brief glimpse of the angel on the other side before the door closed again. Not much of a glimpse—just enough to see a pair of slim legs, topped by a trim rear end.

Not bad. Not bad at all.

There were some muffled exclamations from the hall and he stared up at the ceiling, envisioning the conversation going on between the doctor and ''Emily.'' What a shock to learn your husband doesn't remember you—it would probably be as hard for her as it was for him. The animated discussion went on for some time, but he only caught a few stray words before it ended abruptly.

When the door opened again he swallowed. A second later his eyes opened wide and he grinned with delight.

Wow!

Emily was pure dynamite, with the eyes of an angel and a body that could send him to heaven. Gold hair hung almost to her waist and she wore skimpy shorts and a close-fitting knit top. His gaze settled on her waist. While she was petite otherwise, her tummy was definitely rounded.

A baby? He felt a surge of possessive pride, though his memory remained as blank as before.

"Hi," he said happily, certain there were worse ways to wake up with amnesia.

"Er...Dr. Wescott told me you...uh...can't..."

At the uneasiness in her face he winced. This whole thing was terrible timing. Pregnant women should be treated gently, they didn't need nasty shocks like hearing their husband had amnesia. No matter how shaky things were for him, he wanted to reassure her.

"I'm sorry, I don't remember. But the doctor says it's only temporary." He held out his hand. "Come and give me a kiss. It'll probably come right back."

Emily jumped visibly. "Uh...Nick, are you sure you're not...well...just kidding around?"

He froze. "What?"

"Well, you do like a good joke."

For an instant he felt a flash of dislike for his former self. If his wife thought he'd play a practical joke at such a crucial time for her, then he must have been a jerk. "I'm not kidding," he said quietly. "I can't imagine doing anything so horrible when you're pregnant."

Emily hesitated, stroking her palm over her stomach in a restless gesture that spoke volumes. She probably did that a lot when she was anxious or unhappy, trying to reassure herself that the baby was all right. A soft warmth invaded his heart.

"I mean it. Please kiss me," he whispered.

She edged toward him, obviously nervous. "Nick, you aren't yourself. We should wait till you feel better."

At the moment he felt fine. In fact, he felt like beating on his chest and yelling like Tarzan. Whatever faults his unremembered self suffered from, poor taste in women wasn't one of them. "I just want a kiss," he chided gently. "I didn't ask you to make love to me."

The pink in her cheeks deepened. "I know, I just thought..." She shrugged diffidently.

A stab of frustration turned the corner of his mouth down. He needed Emily to be herself, not so quiet and uneasy. Or was it him? Was he a good husband, or was he terrible? Looking at her, he could well imagine they spent plenty of time in bed, but after that there was a lot of open territory.

Jeez.

He stirred restlessly, kicking at the blanket over his legs, then changed his mind; he didn't have to advertise his physical response to Emily, even if she was his wife. And she'd certainly notice...hospital garments didn't offer much camouflage. He'd have to get something else to wear if he hoped to have some privacy.

"Come here, Angel," he murmured.

Emily stepped to the edge of the bed. Close up she looked even better than across the room. Naturally dark lashes fringed her clear blue eyes, and her skin was smooth and only lightly touched by the sun. The hair he'd thought was gold was more than that—a shimmering array of darks and lights; gold and fiery glints of chestnut. He could already imagine how it would feel, fragrant and cool, sliding against them...between them.

It was rather exciting, the thought of rediscovering lost sensations. Of rediscovering his life. If he didn't remember, it wouldn't be so bad. Everything would be new. Different.

No.

Alarm jolted through him, even worse than when he'd first realized he didn't remember his own name. He was rationalizing, trying to find a good reason not to panic at the thought of never regaining his memory.

Nick.

My name is Nick, he mouthed silently. And this was his wife, Emily. He had a home and family. A baby was on the way. In an hour...or maybe a few days, he'd get things straight in his head and then everything would be fine. It had to be.

"Are you all right?" he asked. The expression in her big, worried eyes troubled him. "Everything's okay with the baby, isn't it? I know this has been a shock."

"Don't worry," she assured him quickly. "My obstetrician is out of town, but Paige...Dr. Wescott gave me a complete examination. I may be little, but I'm tough."

Tough? He fought a ridiculous impulse to smile. "Angel, you look about as tough as a rose petal."

The tip of her tongue flicked over her lips. "Er...you always call me Emily. I don't have any nicknames."

"I like 'Angel,' don't you? It fits. You look like an angel, all pink and gold. You're so beautiful."

"Oh." A look of surprised pleasure erased the worry in her face, yet it increased his own uneasiness. Emily didn't seem accustomed to receiving compliments from him, which meant he must have been blind or insensitive—or both—before the accident. "That's nice...I mean, thank you," she said softly.

He caught her wrist and threaded their fingers together. For the first time he realized there were hard calluses on his hands, which contrasted with the softness of her skin. The small discovery pleased him for some reason.

"What do I do?" he asked. "For a living?"

"You're a civil engineer."

Hmm. It sounded interesting. "Roads, bridges, dams? That kind of thing?"

"Yes. You're out of town a lot, but you're on vacation right now," she explained.

That was a relief. At least he wouldn't have to start evaluating stress tests or any other formula in the immediate future. Stress tests? He thought for a moment and realized there was a lot of highly technical knowledge jumbled in his head. But why was his personal life eluding him?

He pulled on Emily's hand, drawing his reluctant wife closer. He *had* to get his memory back, and if kissing this luscious bundle of femininity would help... Well, it was all for the cause.

Emily looked at Nick, and her toes curled. She'd never seen that particular expression on his face before...a kind of sensual appraisal. *For her.* Awareness flooded her body with startling speed.

Nick thought they were married. *Really* married—not the convenient sort of marriage it actually was. And the doctor said she couldn't tell him, not when the truth was so complicated. It would be too traumatic, especially since he'd heard the medics from the ambulance talking about his wife. For the time being she'd have to pretend they were the perfect, loving couple.

"Come here, Angel," he murmured again, smiling wickedly.

Emily resisted for just a moment. A part of her still believed Nick was playing some sort of elaborate joke and he'd start laughing the minute she came close to kissing him. Marriage or not, they were buddies, not lovers. All her life he'd been like another brother, teasing her in one breath, then tackling the neighborhood bully for calling her a bad name in the next.

Friends.

But there was nothing friendly in the sexy way he kept looking at her...like an ice cream treat on a hot day. With her free hand Emily tugged surreptitiously at her T-shirt, suddenly wishing it was bigger, or that she was wearing some safe, roomy maternity blouse. What was wrong with her? Nick had seen her in a lot less over the years. He'd even seen her in the raw when she was ten— the result of a prank by her obnoxious practical-joke-playing eldest brother.

"Nick," she protested as he drew her down on the hospital bed. "I really don't think this is the...ah...place."

Nick. It sounded a little better now, he decided. He could get used to being called Nick, especially with that breathless way she had of talking. Lifting his arm, he traced the delicate lines of her face, trying to absorb everything as rapidly as possible. Tactile sensations. Physical response. *Anything* to get his memory back.

Emily's skin was soft...he knew that. Like the finest silk. And her lips were moist and velvety. He'd bet they tasted every bit as good as they looked. She had a faintly stubborn line to her jaw, which contrasted adorably with her angelic sweetness.

This was awful.

He couldn't remember being in love with his wife, but he'd immediately fallen into lust. His finger trailed down her throat to the first swell of her breasts, but he hesitated when she trembled.

No, maybe he shouldn't touch her so intimately. Frustration edged along his nerves. *Why couldn't he remember?* For heaven's sake, he felt guilty for touching his own wife. He'd become a stranger. To her. To himself. He didn't know the right touches, the right words, he didn't even know if he was a total, unfeeling, rotten jerk.

"Emily?"

She didn't meet his gaze. "Yes?"

"We're okay, aren't we? I mean, we get along okay, right?"

She smiled a little. "We've always been great friends. We kind of grew up together."

Friends? That didn't tell him very much. He bypassed the tempting curve of her breasts and rested his palm over the swell of her tummy. "When is the baby due?"

Emily swallowed hard. He could even see the muscles working in her throat. "In December," she murmured.

"A Christmas baby. That's nice." With a small shrug to himself, he decided action was better than wondering and worrying. With a smooth, unhurried motion he drew her across his body.

Emily gasped, but didn't fight him.

Grinning, he twisted until she rested on the pillow and he could arch over her, his back to the door to give them some privacy. It felt great, even though his abused muscles protested. Rebellion simmered in her blue eyes and a healthy flush of annoyance brightened her skin. *Good.* He didn't want her to hide her emotions—he'd never remember a thing about their life if she didn't act like herself around him.

"Mad at me, Angel?"

"Whatever gave you that idea?" Emily's bottom lip pouted out, and he raised an eyebrow.

"I'm not sure, but it might be that not-so-angelic glare on your face."

"I told you, I don't have any nicknames. I've never been called an angel in my life."

"I still like it…Angel." Ignoring her muffled shriek of protest, he eased his fingers into the shiny thickness of her hair, concentrating on the texture of the cool silken strands. It occurred to him that he ought to be a little less confident—at least for someone whose memory resembled Swiss cheese—but he was enjoying himself too much.

"Let go of me."

"Uh-uh. I want to kiss my wife."

Emily gulped as he kissed her forehead. It wasn't the first time Nick had touched her, she reminded herself. She would just pretend this was like any other platonic hug they'd shared. With this decision in mind, she closed her eyes and waited for the "kiss."

His laugh was little more than a tremor of movement in his chest. "Going to take your medicine like a good girl?"

Her eyes flew open, flashing blue sparks. *That* was the old Nick. *That* was Nick Carleton playing one of his friendly I'm-almost-like-family jokes. Most of the time it wasn't too bad, but this time he'd gone too far!

Chapter Two

Emily glowered. Some joke.

Amnesia? She'd give Nick worse than amnesia, she'd put him in traction!

"Why you arrogant wretch! I knew you were—"

Her furious diatribe was smothered by Nick's mouth, hot and open over her own, possessive, his tongue invading her inner softness. On second thought, this wasn't at *all* like the Nicholas Carleton she knew. Surely he wouldn't go to this length for a gag...kissing her so passionately?

If he was fooling, it was an incredible acting job. Emily moaned, the assault on her senses threatening logical deduction.

No, he had to be fooling.

With that thought in mind, Emily drew up her knee to teach Mr. I'm Almost Like Family a lesson he wouldn't quickly forget. It was then she realized she had proof of something Nick couldn't fake, and certainly wouldn't *feel* if he was just joking. He was leaning over her, pressing his weight along the side of her body. A sheet and blanket covered his hips, but they couldn't disguise the bold, hard power of his arousal. Her heart skipped into triple time.

"Nick...?"

"Shhh." His thumb traced her collarbone. "God, Emily. You smell so good...feel so good. I can't wait until I get out of here. I must be the luckiest man in town. Why can't I remember?"

Emily gulped, torn by the pain and frustration in his voice. Their friendship was too special to lose—he'd be horribly embarrassed when his memory came back. Imagine, passionately kissing the woman you'd always treated like a kid sister. And what about when she had to take him home from the hospital?

Home...as in a normal marriage with a shared bed.

The breath caught in her throat as Nick's hand slid lower, carefully cupping her breast. Surprised response spun outward, clenching her abdomen.

"N...no!" She stuttered, pushing his fingers away and fumbling at the hospital bed railing. This was crazy. It was just shock and uncertainty making her respond to his touch. She couldn't want to sleep with him, could she? Her best friend?

She had to get away, to think.

"Angel...Emily, stop it," Nick protested, trying to halt her frantic motions as she hung over the side, searching for something to grab on to. "What's wrong? What did I do?"

At that moment the railing dropped, and Emily slipped, falling toward the floor. Fear swamped all her other emotions.

No! The baby.

With a desperate lunge Nick caught her, the alarm in

his face mirroring her own. He dragged her back onto the mattress, swearing a blue streak.

For several seconds Emily lay quietly, breathlessly listening to her heart thud and her husband curse. But when he reached the fifth "dammit all to hell" she'd had enough.

"Quiet!" She wiggled into a semiupright position. "Don't you dare use that kind of language in front of my baby."

"It's my kid, too!"

The sound of laughter startled them both. They turned toward the door and saw a grinning Dr. Wescott. "Good catch, Nick. I see you're getting back to normal."

"I'm fine." He crossed his arms and glared at Emily. "But it's no wonder I can't remember my name, my wife probably scared it out of me."

"I did nothing of the sort. You fell off the roof."

The doctor laughed again. "You both seem accident prone. I guess it's a match made in heaven."

"Thanks a lot," Emily muttered.

At the moment she could cheerfully strangle Paige Wescott. She should have known better than to choose an old school chum for a doctor. Of course, no one could have predicted Nick would fall off the roof and develop a highly inconvenient case of memory loss.

She carefully brushed her hair from her face, ignoring Nick, who seemed to be handling amnesia a lot better than he deserved. The wretch.

"Are you all right, Angel?" he asked.

"Lord," she muttered. "You must ask me that a dozen times a day."

He scowled at her. "Of course I do. Remember me? The husband? Just because *I* can't remember doesn't mean I don't have a stake in you, or the baby."

Emily bit her lip, ashamed of the way she'd reacted. Nick wasn't himself. He'd awakened without a memory, knowing only that he had a wife, without remembering the unusual circumstances of their marriage. Sheesh, what a mess.

"He's right. I'd better check you over again, just to be sure," Paige said, still standing at the open doorway with an amused expression on her face. "They'll be coming to take Nick for more tests, anyway."

"I feel fine, Doc," Nick interjected.

"That's good. But we'll keep you here for a while, just to be sure." The physician looked at Emily, still tangled with him on the bed. "Coming?"

"Coming," Emily muttered. She carefully swung her feet to the floor and received an affectionate pat on her bottom from "the husband." She gave him a fulminating glance. Amnesia or not, Nick had better watch his hands.

Grinning, Nick watched the two women leave, then tucked his hands behind his head and gazed out the hospital window.

Nicholas Carleton.

Nick.

He turned the name over and over in his mind, yet it didn't seem any more familiar than it had before.

Nick. My name is Nicholas Carleton.

In a short period of time he'd pieced together several parts of his missing life. Most of it looked pretty good. Some of it he wasn't so sure about. Let's see....

Wife? Emily Carleton. Pregnant, saucy and delectable. A definite plus. She might not be an angel, but she got full points in every other category.

Career? Civil engineer, but on vacation. That wasn't too bad, either.

Home? Presumably a house with a leaky roof—unless he'd been cleaning rain gutters and fell off that way. That made the house a question mark. But if he lived there with Emily it couldn't be too awful. He already knew Emily could brighten up any place.

Character...?

Hmm. Frowning, he shifted uneasily. He didn't like the astonished way his wife had responded to his compliments, or her belief he might be playing a practical joke. And what about the baby? She'd said, "Don't you dare use that kind of language in front of my baby."

Not *our* baby, but *my* baby.

What did that mean...if it meant anything? Were they having trouble in their marriage?

A needle of alarm stabbed through his already aching head. He shouldn't have teased her so much. Deep down he realized he'd been hiding how terrible he felt inside—lost, alone, as though he was standing on the edge of a precipice with nothing but darkness around him. It had been stupid and insensitive, and had almost resulted in Emily getting hurt herself.

A wave of nausea rolled over him as he recalled the moment when she'd started to fall. He slumped deeper into the bed. The facts he'd gathered didn't matter—he still didn't know who he really was, or what kind of man he'd been. There was only one thing he was absolutely certain about...Emily loved and wanted their child.

Surely that meant she loved him a little, too.

Didn't it?

"I'll be fine," Emily said, thanking the deputy sheriff as she got out of the cruiser.

"I'm sure Nick'll get over this amnesia stuff real quick. Just call if you have any more problems." Hank McAllister tipped his hat.

Emily sighed. Everyone had been so nice and helpful. It was a great hospital. The nurses had gotten her food, insisting she eat. Then Hank, an old high school pal of Nick and her brother, had come to take her home. There hadn't been anyone else to call: most of her friends were on vacation, her folks had retired to Arizona, her sisters and younger brother lived out of state, and her real big brother was somewhere in Wyoming or Montana fighting forest fires. Or maybe Idaho.

Frazzled, she wandered into the living room and sank onto the couch.

So far she'd handled her pregnancy easily; no morning sickness, no particular aches and pains or hormonal swings. None of the emotional roller coaster rides her yuppie married-with-children friends had warned her about. She absolutely *loved* being pregnant. It was the best thing that had ever happened to her.

The soft tick-tock of the mantel clock was the only discernible sound in the house, that and the dripping water faucet Nick had planned to fix after finishing the roof.

Nick.... Emily curled into a ball and burst into tears. "How did it happen?" she moaned into the cushions.

Everything had been going so perfectly. She was going to have a baby. She'd always wanted kids, and it seemed somehow perfect that Nick would be the father. Sure, getting used to the idea had taken a little while, then everything had fallen into place.

Their marriage hadn't changed anything. She still took care of his mail and paid his bills when he was out of town. And he was out of town a lot. Nick consulted on projects all over the world. Whenever he did come home he'd cadge meals at her place and sheepishly hand her a bag of laundry in the bargain. Big difference getting married had made.

Now she had a husband with amnesia—an *amorous* husband with amnesia—who didn't have any idea they were only friends. And the worst part was knowing how much she'd responded to him. Incredibly. Passionately. Melting like a chocolate bar in his hands. How could they go back to being just friends?

"Mrrooow!"

Opening her eyes, she found herself nose to nose with her cat. "Oh. Hi, GeeZee." She sniffed.

A rough tongue lapped at the tears on her cheeks. She moved to give the enormous, black-and-white feline room by her side. His booming purr soothed her, and she cuddled him close. "We'll have to rearrange the house a little. We have to make it look like Nick lives here," she muttered. "Paige says we can't upset him with the truth."

Emily wiggled, hoping to get more comfortable so she could take a nap. GeeZee merowled and gave her a disgusted look, so she scratched his neck and tried to relax. An hour later she was still awake. Exhausted, but awake.

"Blast."

According to the clock it was almost five in the afternoon. Nick had fallen off the roof less than eight hours before…it seemed like forever ago. Her life had changed a lot in those hours. Now she had to act like a dutiful, loving wife. Ick, *dutiful*. Except it wasn't the dutiful part that bothered her the most.

GeeZee stretched luxuriously and bumped her with his forehead. She sighed. "You're so big. You can't sleep

on the bed when Nick gets here. There won't be enough
room.''

For a full twenty seconds Emily froze, her words
echoing in her ears. *There won't be enough room.* She
gulped and scrambled inelegantly off the couch.

"Arggh! I can't believe I said that. Nick and I won't
be sleeping together. He doesn't have his memory and
he's always been oversexed, but that doesn't mean I'm
going to fall into line like all his other women. No way.
Not me. I'll do laundry and meals, but the horizontal
mambo—or whatever those bachelors call it—is out.
Marriage or not.''

GeeZee stared at her without blinking, as though he
thought a strange spirit had come and taken the place of
his normally sensible human.

Emily stomped back and forth across the living room,
gesturing wildly. "I'm going to make it clear to Nick.
He'll be grateful when he finally remembers. He doesn't
actually want to make love to me. It's that old 'glad I'm
alive' survival response. Primitive instinct. That's all. It
has nothing to do with me whatsoever.''

Having clearly decided this was the case, she looked
at herself in the mirror above the fireplace and burst into
tears again. "I'm fat. I'm pregnant with his baby and he
doesn't *really* want me because I'm fat.''

It took her ten minutes of crying, twenty minutes in
the shower, and a whole lot of self-lecturing before she
could even begin to think straight. And then she still had
to get dressed for evening visiting hours at the hospital.

Emily toweled her wet hair vigorously. "Big deal,''
she mumbled. "I'm fat because I'm pregnant. That's a
great reason to be fat. I'll just wear a maternity dress so
it's really obvious I'm having a baby.''

Still dissatisfied, she looked at her reflection again.

Wonderful. Nick was going to know she'd gone home and bawled her head off. But it was just those pesky hormones, finally showing up after over four and a half months of pregnancy.

Well...why not? She'd always been a late bloomer, why should her pregnancy be any different?

Clean, properly clothed, with her emotions firmly under control, Emily drove back to the hospital. Paige Wescott met her in the hallway, and she looked at the physician hopefully.

"He still doesn't have his memory," Paige warned.

"This is crazy. Somebody will slip and tell him the truth," Emily declared. "We should tell him first."

"Oh? Who's going to tell him? Just how many people know you had artificial insemination? Or that Nick isn't something special in your life? Or that you don't have a regular marriage?"

Emily blinked. "He must have told his friends."

Paige clucked. "Nick is a man. I doubt he told anyone the details of your baby's conception, especially his friends. Since it's clear he's the father, I suspect he's letting everyone believe the obvious. What do you think?"

A vivid image of Nick's embarrassed face rose before Emily's eyes. He was a nice guy—with Neanderthal tendencies. Positively primeval. He'd no more discuss the intimate details of their trip to the gynecologist's office, than he'd rob a bank.

But even more than that, Emily knew she hadn't been entirely...well, *candid* herself. Crockett, Washington, was a small town, with its full share of affectionately wagging tongues. While she hadn't exactly *lied* to anyone, she hadn't really explained about the baby. Or Nick.

She'd even taken his last name since she never planned to remarry and because it would be easier for their child.

"Well?" Paige prodded.

"All right," she agreed reluctantly. "Except I can't keep the pretense up forever. I'm no good at it. I feel so guilty about yelling at him and pushing him away. What if he never gets his memory back because of me? And he's just going to die if he remembers. He'll wake up and say 'yuck, I kissed Emily. I knew her when she was a skinny eight-year-old with bubble gum in her braces.'"

Paige shook her head. "Hormones," she complained. "Look, I'm not an expert on amnesia, but I do know Nick. And so do you. His personality is so close to the surface his memory block is transparent."

"What has that got to do with anything?"

"That means," the doctor said patiently, "my instincts say you should treat him like you always would—argue, tease, whatever...except you don't explain about your marriage. He latched on to the idea of being married like a drowning victim clutching a life preserver. Under the circumstances, I can't say I blame him. Don't worry, he'll remember soon enough."

"When is that going to happen?"

"It shouldn't be long. I suspect this is a case of selective amnesia. His injuries were minor, so the memory block must be caused by some emotional conflict."

Emily blinked again. Nick Carleton emotionally conflicted? Interesting. Not overly helpful, but interesting.

"You're the only anchor he's got right now," Paige said seriously. "You've been friends since childhood. I doubt there's anyone as close to him. The treatment in these cases is fairly simple—get him into familiar surroundings, remind him of his life, and his memory should return. From what you've said, he spends more time at your house than he ever does at that apartment in the city.''

"But he thinks we're...we're really involved. I mean, uh, Nick has never kissed me like that before,'' Emily said, flustered.

"From what I saw, it's about time he did.'' With that parting shot Paige patted her arm and headed toward the nurse's station.

"God save me from matchmakers,'' Emily muttered. She pushed open the door of Nick's room with a nervous smile, smoothing the light cotton skirt of her dress.

Nick rose from his chair, relieved to see Emily instead of another doctor or lab technician, who would just be annoyed because he'd gotten out of bed. Although...he'd be happy to see her no matter what. "Hi, Angel. I wasn't sure if you'd come back tonight.''

"Of course I'd come back.'' She took a few steps into the room. "How's your head?''

"Empty,'' he said flatly. "It's like there's this enormous wall in my mind and I can't see over it.''

"I'm sorry.''

He winced. Great, he had to act like a bear with a sore paw. This was his wife, not a stranger. He was lucky to have Emily, it would have been far worse waking up without anybody to care about him. Which reminded him...

"Angel, what about my family? If you haven't called them yet, maybe you should wait. I'm sure I'll get my memory back soon, so there's no need to upset them, too.''

A look of genuine dismay flashed into her eyes, and he leaned forward abruptly.

Yikes. His abused head didn't appreciate the movement, but it seemed more important to understand why Emily might be upset. Even worse...he could tell she'd been crying. "Angel? What's wrong?"

"Nothing. Except...you don't have a family." Her voice shook and she didn't quite meet his gaze.

"Wrong," he said quietly. "I have you and the baby."

Instinctively Emily's hand went to her stomach. He went to her, grateful a supposed old friend from the fire department had sent a pair of pajamas for him to wear. She jumped a little when he put an arm about her waist and led her to the bed.

"Is there something I should know?" he asked, sitting her down beside him. "It can't be too terrible—you said we practically grew up together."

"We did."

Emily fidgeted with the fabric of her sundress. It was pretty and feminine, her smooth shoulders rising above the fitted bodice. Her pregnancy was concealed by the graceful folds of the skirt, but he would have preferred seeing the evidence of their baby. It made him feel alive and potent, very much a man.

He captured her fingers, pressing both their hands against her abdomen. "So?"

"We grew up here in Crockett," she murmured, her head still bowed. "Your mother and father are dead—you were raised in a foster home next door to us."

"Who is us?"

"My parents and brothers and sisters." She cast him a look from the corner of her eye. "You're great friends with my oldest brother. You practically lived at our place."

"What about my foster parents, are we close? Do I see them ever?" When Emily didn't answer right away he kissed the arched curve of her neck. "Don't protect me, Angel. I have to know."

"They weren't unkind," Emily whispered. "They kept you warm and fed and dry."

And that's all. Nick didn't need her to finish the story for him, he'd already guessed. Whatever affection he'd received as a child must have been from Emily and her own family. No wonder he'd fallen in love with her.

"We've never really discussed it," Emily said, finally lifting her head. "You don't like to talk about things like that."

You don't like to talk about things like that.... Terrific. Now he had another item to add to the growing list of questions about himself. But surely he confided in Emily. She was his wife, and she was also the kind of woman who'd want a close relationship with her husband. Besides, marriage meant partnership, didn't it?

The sudden intake of her breath grabbed his attention. "What? Is something wrong?"

"Did you feel that?" she asked excitedly. "The baby moved." She squirmed until she could clasp both her hands over his, holding him to the firm swell of her belly. "It's the first time I've felt anything."

Awed, Nick realized there was a flutter of movement beneath his palm. A faint, compelling reminder of growing life.

"Isn't it wonderful?" Emily asked, tears welling in her blue eyes.

Uh-oh. Uncertain about the best thing to do, he cuddled her close. He didn't know the cause—the accident, fear or just plain happiness over their baby. He doubted she cried very often. "It's all right," he soothed.

"Drat. I thought I was over this." She sniffed and

gulped. "It's just hormones. They all attacked at once. I was doing fine until today."

"I see."

"I don't cry, not ever," she said, her stubborn chin raised high.

"I know." Nick wiped the damp streaks from her cheeks, and she gave him a wobbly smile. God, she was so desirable. Without even thinking he lifted her face and kissed her.

It was even better than the first time. She was soft and fragrant, still trembling with emotion and excitement. After a long moment she moaned and held him in return. He could easily have forgotten they were in a hospital, but for the emphatic sound of someone clearing their throat.

"Nick...Emily?"

He almost swore, recalling just in time that Emily didn't like that kind of language around their baby. She must believe in that "influence from the womb" theory of psychology. Nick felt an instant of supreme, absolute frustration—how could he remember a psychology theory and remember nothing tangible about his own wife?

"You have lousy timing, Doc. *Again*," he growled. Regretfully, he brushed a last kiss across Emily's lips before releasing her. "How do I break out of this prison, anyhow?"

Paige Wescott shrugged, her smile growing wider as she watched a flustered Emily straighten her clothing. "A specialist is coming from Seattle to check you over, but you'll probably be released tomorrow or the next day."

"How about a temporary release?" he suggested, smoothing his hand over Emily's shoulder, covered only

by a one-inch strap. "You release me tonight, and I'll
come back in the morning. I promise."

Paige seemed to be having trouble controlling her expression, and Emily glared at her. "I...uh...that's not
such a good idea. You haven't been cleared for extra-
curricular activities."

"Nick, I've been meaning to talk to you about that,"
Emily said. "I don't think—"

"Wait a minute." Frowning, Nick ran his thumb over
her ring finger—her *bare* ring finger. "Where's your
wedding ring?"

"Um...at home. I took it off because I was baking
cookies." Emily wanted to die. The truth was, there
wasn't any wedding ring. Nick had wanted to buy one,
but she hadn't let him because it had seemed silly under
the circumstances.

"You took it off?"

Emily looked at him carefully, yet she couldn't be
sure if it was reproach or uncertainty in his face. She
decided a direct attack was called for, if only to distract
him. "Yes. But you don't wear *your* ring, either."

Nick glanced down at his own hand, still frowning.
He clenched his fingers into a brief, tight fist. "I'll have
to change that. How long have we been married?"

Emily's heart speeded up. She knew the answers to
his questions, it just seemed so strange to hear *Nick* asking such things. In some ways he knew her better than
anyone else. "A little over five months."

Five months? Nick whistled to himself, rather pleased
with the knowledge. "We sure didn't waste any time.
You must have gotten pregnant right away."

"Yes, it's August 21 now," Dr. Wescott said deliberately. "The baby is due December 30th."

Nick groaned. "I don't need to be told the

date...*again.*'' He turned to his wife and shrugged. ''They keep repeating the date and what town I live in—all kinds of stuff. I think the doc pulled out an old psych textbook and is experimenting on me.''

He gently stroked Emily's back and rubbed her neck.

''You're lucky,'' Paige retorted. ''A hundred years ago we would have just hit you over the head again.'' She looked at Emily. ''I forgot to tell you to come by my office before you leave. You're under a lot of stress—I want you to take some extra vitamins for a few days.''

Nick shook his head after the doctor walked out. It hadn't taken him long to get tired of hospital life. Not that he had much ability to make comparisons in view of his faulty memory.

''Nick...we have to talk,'' Emily said. Before he could stop her she slid out of his reach and into a nearby chair.

''Okay. What about?''

Emily pursed her lips, trying to decide the best way to tell Nick that they'd be sleeping separately, no matter *when* he got home.

''I don't think we should be intimate. Not right away,'' she said quickly. ''It would be best...for both of us. Don't you think?'' She cringed at the last question. Giving Nick an option wasn't what she'd had in mind.

''Anyway,'' she continued. ''I'm in a awkward stage right now with the baby. Being together...'' A wild heat flooded Emily's face and she faltered. ''It's difficult...and my stomach gets upset so easily. And...and with everything that's happened, it would be better to take things slowly. You know, get settled into a routine.''

He leaned back on one arm, his face expressionless.

"Nick?"

"Okay. We'll take things one day at a time," he agreed calmly—a lot more calmly than she'd really expected. "This has been as tough for you as it is for me. Tougher probably." Then he smiled, a slow, sexy, hot smile. A smile that infuriated her all the more because it said he was just humoring his overly emotional, pregnant wife. "Don't worry, it'll be all right when we get home, Angel."

I'm not your angel, and I'm trying to save you from major embarrassment, she shouted silently. But her protest did nothing to stop the flow of sensual heat sliding through her veins.

I can't believe this. I've known Nick for more than twenty-five years. I can't be feeling this way. For years I've teased him about his little black book and all those women parading through his life. He was even voted "most likely to escape the ball and chain" by his high school senior class.

Boy, she thought darkly, he'd thought that was funny.

"Think about it," Nick continued. "You're just uneasy because I can't remember us being married. I bet you feel it's like I'm being unfaithful, even though it's my own wife I want to make love to."

Her jaw sagged. *That's it!* Time to follow Paige's advice. Act normally. She'd never let Nick get away with a statement like that if he was himself.

She opened her mouth, "I think they call that kind of idiocy psycho-babble. *Honey.*"

Okay, Nick decided, he was wrong. That wasn't the reason Emily wanted to keep him at arm's length. But he was tired of trying to understand every stray glance, every uncomfortable pause, every peculiar comment people made around him. It was altogether likely they had a wonderful marriage, with no real problems. He had to believe that. Hell, he *needed* to believe that.

Maybe he'd been a jerk and teased her about getting bigger because of the baby—she'd already hinted that he had a dubious sense of humor. And there was the issue of trust. He didn't remember their relationship, so she didn't know how he'd act. It was like asking her to be intimate with a virtual stranger.

"And by the way—" Emily crossed her arms "—I really hate it when you're condescending. *So cut it out.*"

Phew. Emily was wonderfully sweet and spicy, but the spicy part was obviously in control tonight. No wonder. He suspected she felt vulnerable and worried and was striking out in self-defense.

"Think of this as the ideal opportunity to expose my faults and correct them," he suggested.

Emily wanted to throw something at him. Blast. Yet it really wasn't Nick who was the problem. It was her. She could excuse his behavior because he didn't remember their friendship. But she didn't have any excuse for herself. She'd *wanted* him to kiss her. She'd wanted him to want the baby...

All at once Emily felt the blood drain from her face. *Of course.* No matter how much she told Nick the baby was hers, that he didn't need to feel responsible...she had hoped he would share this incredible thing with her.

"I...I have to go see Paige," she stuttered, getting to her feet and backing toward the door.

Nick stiffened. "What's wrong?"

"Wrong? N-nothing." She rubbed her throat with the back of her hand. "It's okay. It's just those hormones, you know?"

"Wait." Nick caught her at the door. "I'm sorry for

teasing. I'd give anything to make this easier on you. You know that, don't you?''

Emily's chest rose and fell with shaky breaths. His eyes were so sincere, so filled with loving and latent passion she wanted to melt like warm honey. Only she couldn't let herself want him. Their friendship was already in jeopardy. When he remembered...could they ever put the pieces back together again?

She escaped as quickly as possible. And because she was already feeling illogical and emotional, she stormed into Paige's office with all the temperamental energy her battered emotions would allow.

"Thanks a lot," she snapped.

Paige leaned back in her chair and crossed her arms. "I didn't give him amnesia."

"You told me to act like his wife."

"You *are* his wife."

"Legally."

"Well, legally you signed the admission papers to the hospital. You authorized treatment. You told 911 your *husband* fell off the roof. You established yourself as the man's wife in just about every way a woman can." Her friend's voice was relentless, refusing to let her deny anything.

Swallowing, Emily leaned against the bookshelf filled with medical references, needing the solid support her world had lost. "What can I do? How do I get out of this?''

Paige's expression softened with sympathy and understanding—and a little mischief. "I don't know. But I've seen how attentive he can be. Are you sure you want the old Nick back?''

Chapter Three

Are you sure you want the old Nick back?

Muttering beneath her breath, Emily stopped at the door of Nick's apartment and searched her purse for the key. Trust Paige to raise doubts where none should exist. And the rest of their conversation hadn't helped, either.

There's never been anything between us except friendship. I don't want to lose that.

Even for something better?

Better?

As in love? Emily shook her head, remembering Paige's earnest question. What a joke. After her first shot at romantic marriage, she knew friendship was the preferable choice.

Nick was always there when she needed him—he'd even come back from a bridge-building project in South America when she'd called and asked if he knew anyone who could break Kevin's kneecaps. Of course, she hadn't really been serious about the kneecaps, but he'd come back, anyway, to make sure she stayed out of jail…and that she filed for divorce.

Though when Nick had learned *everything,* he'd blown a gasket and almost ended up with his own assault charge. Emily shivered as she remember the cold rage in his eyes and the way he'd stood between her and Kevin on the courthouse steps…Kevin and his smarmy, "Sorry 'bout things, babe, can't we try again?"

Try again? He hadn't tried in the first place, he'd just wanted her to come back to the advertising firm where they'd both worked and to keep giving him her ideas.

"Hello, *gorg*eous," a man's voice said from behind her. "I think Nick's out of town, but I'm available."

Another smarmy type. Yuck.

"I'm not." She found the key and jammed it into the lock before turning so that her full profile was visible. The slick yuppie's eyes widened as he observed her tummy. He stuttered an apology and speedily backed into his own apartment.

"Good," Emily muttered. She swung the door open and wrinkled her nose. She always expected Nick's place to smell like Seattle—a kind of piney, salty fragrance, mixed with the inevitable scent of a city. But it didn't. It just smelled dead. Probably because he was out of town so much of the time.

She preferred Crockett, which clung to the western edge of Puget Sound like a barnacle in the midst of a sprawling sea of tide pools. No one ever paid much attention to Crockett, which was fine, because Crockett didn't care. Who needed rising real estate costs, minimalls and factory outlet stores? You could get all that in Seattle, which was only a short drive and ferry ride away.

The specialist had arrived early that morning, clucked

and examined Nick to the absolute limit of his annoyance. The doctor had decided there wasn't anything organically wrong causing the memory block, concurring with the selective amnesia theory. But he fancied things up by calling it "dissociative amnesia." And, without necessarily agreeing with Paige Wescott's treatment, he'd said they would have to continue letting Nick believe he had a typical marriage for the time being. Which didn't surprise Emily, since the good doctor obviously had some trouble believing the truth himself.

Apparently amnesia was unpredictable and every case was different. Nobody completely agreed on how to treat the condition, but everybody was fascinated by it.

"Blast," she muttered as she began gathering Nick's belongings.

Clothes for Nick weren't a big problem. He subscribed to a style best described as "casual" and "more casual." She stuffed a bunch of jeans, shirts and underwear into a duffel bag. Those—with the clothing he always kept in Crockett—would be plenty.

As for personal items?

Emily frowned as she looked around the apartment. It looked like a hotel room. She'd never thought about that before, except in passing, as a point to tease Nick about.

After twenty minutes of searching, Emily found a modest collection of mementos. It still wouldn't look like Nick *really* lived in her house, but for that matter, his apartment didn't look too lived in, either.

Emily yawned and looked at her watch. It would have to do. She made two trips to her Chevy Blazer in the parking lot and then climbed into the driver's seat with a sigh. For the first time in her life, the ferry ride from Bremerton had made her queasy. She didn't look for-

ward to another one quite so soon, but she had a lot to
do before Nick came "home."

The next morning Emily found Nick striding down
the hospital hallway to meet her, dressed in borrowed
pajamas and a navy silk robe. He gave her a lopsided
grin. Aside from the minuscule bandage over his forehead that emphasized his tanned skin, he looked absolutely fit. And perfectly normal, except for the warm
intent in his eyes.

"Angel." Catching her in his arms, Nick covered her
mouth greedily.

"Nick," she murmured between slow, open kisses
that seemed to last forever. "Paige said—"

"Shhh."

Memory or not, Nick was still an opportunist. He slid
his tongue between her parted lips, invading her mouth
so deeply Emily didn't know where either of them began
or ended. A whole field of butterflies began fluttering in
her stomach, and she almost dropped the plastic shopping bag she carried.

When he released her finally, reluctantly, he gave her
a smile of happy contentment. "Hi, Angel. I'm getting
sprung this morning. Isn't that great?"

Emily gulped, feeling so light-headed she clung to his
arm for support. *Lack of oxygen* she decided. Maybe that
was how Nick got his women in bed—he cut off their
oxygen with those long kisses until they didn't have any
more resistance. Not that they'd resist much…Nick had
an easy, relaxed, sexy charm that turned generally sensible women into drooling harem mates. She stifled a
scowl.

Drat.

Emily shook her head, trying to dispel images she had

no basis for believing. Did Nick *really* have all those
women she razzed him about? There hadn't been evidence of rampant womanizing in his apartment—no fla-
vored body lotions, no stash of fine wines, no condoms
in every convenient location. Not that she'd really
looked for things like that, but nothing had jumped out
at her, either.

"Angel?" Nick's strong fingers cupped her chin and
jaw. "Don't you want me to come home?"

Oh, dear. He'd misinterpreted her silence. Emily gave
him a reassuring smile. Whatever else happened, Nick
was her dearest friend in the world. "Of course I do."
She held up the shopping bag. "I even brought you a
change of clothes. I just hope it's not too soon. You
scared me."

He continued to stare into her upturned face, absently
stroking his thumbs across her lips. Small shivers ran
down her body. He kept doing that—not wanting her far
from his touch, and never out of his sight. He'd seemed
upset each time she left the hospital for an errand, and
obviously she couldn't explain about needing to buy
wedding rings or getting his belongings from the city.

"You're pale today," Nick murmured, "I know you
don't like me asking, but are you all right?"

Emily swallowed, remembering the bout of morning
sickness she'd experienced earlier. No wonder, after rid-
ing the ferry and getting upset over his accident and
having her hormones attack...and everything. She had
every excuse in the world to have some morning sickness, even if most women didn't *start* tossing their cookies halfway through their second trimester.

"Just...uh...you know." She motioned to her stomach and Nick's hand drifted downward, grazing her
breasts and then resting securely on her abdomen.

Warmth seeped through the thin cotton of her dress, and her breathing quickened.

"I'll be there the next time. I'll help you," he promised.

Help her? Emily would have smiled if her nerves hadn't been so jumpy. Nick was a wonderful pal. He helped with repairs on the house or worked on her car. And it had nothing to do with their so-called marriage. Nick might tease or cheerfully complain, but she could count on him. On the other hand, she couldn't imagine him coping with nausea or roller-coaster hormones.

Emily looked into Nick's brown eyes and felt her heart take a slow, skipping turn. His gaze burned with a kind of hungry, proud, tender expression that was as old as Adam and Eve.

The baby, she thought. *He's acting this way because of the baby.*

The corners of her mouth trembled.

For once, she'd like it to be for her. For once she'd like to be the center of someone's world. To share the loving and giving. She'd tried it once...with Kevin, but she hadn't realized Kevin didn't know the slightest thing about loving and giving. Her marriage had been an absolute disaster.

Maybe it wouldn't be a disaster with Nick.

Lord. Things were getting out of hand. *She* was getting out of hand...completely nuts. When Nick got his memory back they'd be lucky to stay friends. And it would be even worse if she let things between them go beyond kissing.

"Angel? Tell me what's wrong," Nick said, concern creasing his forehead.

"Nothing is wrong. It's just weird," she murmured, "not having you remember me."

"A part of me remembers," Nick whispered, a wicked twinkle creeping into his eyes as he widened his stance and pulled her closer.

"I don't mean *that*," Emily said, annoyed. She tried to pretend it didn't matter that Nick was aroused, and that he was unabashedly letting her feel what "part" he "remembered." She wiggled out of his arms and took two steps backward. "You...*we're* in a public hospital."

"Not for long," said Paige Wescott as she walked down the corridor toward them. She grinned at the flustered Emily and looked Nick over carefully. "I see you're doing okay."

"Get me out of here and I'll do a lot better, Doc," he said with a wink.

"Fine," Paige said, smiling as though she didn't know everything...like the fact that Nick and Emily didn't have a regular marriage with matched sets of pillowcases and slippers under the same bed. Which of course she *did* know.

Emily fumed. She turned her head away from Nick and glared at Paige. "Don't you think he should limit his activities for a while?" she asked pointedly.

"Nonsense," Nick said before Paige could pass judgment. "I talked to that specialist when he was here yesterday. He said I could resume my normal life."

Swell. Emily could hardly explain the "normal" life he was so eager to resume didn't exist. And Paige thought the whole thing was riotously funny. Which only went to prove that Nick was the only real friend she had, except he couldn't remember a thing, the dope.

"Dr. Finn is an excellent doctor," Paige murmured, sounding very diplomatic.

Nick eased his left hand through the silken thickness of Emily's hair, trying not to worry about his wife's uneasy reaction each time he touched her. The winking gold of his wedding ring was no competition for the shimmering, rich color of her hair, but he was still glad to see it. Emily's ring, too. He supposed the two bands looked so new because they hadn't been married for very long.

Damn.

A vague uneasiness kept creeping into his mind...a suspicion that everything wasn't right. Like now. Emily was clearly hesitant about resuming the intimate aspects of their marriage. It might be exactly what she'd said— a temporary discomfort because of the baby. After all, her body was going through a lot of changes. On the other hand, it might be something worse. It might be *him.* Was he an awful lover? Insensitive?

If that was the case, he intended to remedy the situation immediately. Emily deserved the best—the best husband, the best father for her baby, and certainly the best lover.

But what if it was something else? The problem didn't have to be sex, it could be anything. The possibilities were endless. What kind of fool could he have been to let his marriage get messed up? It was hard to imagine getting his memory back and finding out he *didn't* want Emily.

"—get dressed and Emily can complete the paper-work."

"Huh?" He looked blankly at Dr. Wescott, realizing he'd missed part of the conversation during his uncomfortable self-questioning.

"Are you all right, Nick?" The physician's voice held a crisp edge of professionalism. "Do you have a head-ache?"

"No, I'm fine. I was just thinking."

"Did you remember something?" Emily asked, a curious mixture of excitement and regret on her face. Regret? Worry dug deeper into Nick's stomach.

"Not a thing," he said, rather grimly. *Remembering* was getting more and more important...to both of them. He only hoped the *remembering* would be a little less of a shock than the forgetting had been. "I just want to get out of here."

"Fine. You get dressed, and we'll sign you out immediately." Dr. Wescott gave him another one of her reassuring smiles.

He hated those smiles—not because he didn't like Paige Wescott, but because they meant he was still a patient and being treated with kid gloves. At least she'd stopped repeating the date constantly. She must have felt as ridiculous as he did hearing "it's August 21," then "August 22," over and over again.

Nick took the bag Emily had brought him and went to his room. The clothes were casual and comfortable. But not familiar. Nothing seemed familiar except Emily. Her sweet and spicy personality was the only thing that felt right.

Several times during the past two nights he'd looked at the mirror, hoping to recognize himself. It hadn't helped. He saw a man in his mid to late thirties, with thick brown hair and brown eyes. Small lines at the corners of his eyes made him look as if he smiled a lot. He seemed to have a lot of muscles, and his restlessness suggested he preferred an active lifestyle.

Some help.

The jeans he'd been wearing when he'd entered the hospital hadn't reassured him any. In fact, they'd disturbed him more than ever. His valuables had gone home with Emily that first night—a wallet, a sturdy watch on a worn leather band and car keys. No big deal. But in the pocket of the jeans he'd found a matchbook from a place called El Flamenco, with the name Carmen scribbled on it, next to some numbers. The numbers looked like a foreign exchange code for the phone.

Carmen.

A tap on the door rescued him from the unpleasant conjecture he'd been cheating on Emily. Surely he wouldn't have done anything so contemptible—or so stupid.

"Come in." Nick finished tying the laces on his shoes and looked up to see Dr. Wescott.

"Ready to go? Emily's getting the car."

Nick thought rapidly. Paige appeared to be a good friend of Emily's, maybe she could help him. "Uh...Doc, about Emily..." His voice trailed as he tried to think of a good way to say his own wife didn't want to have sex with him, and to ask her advice on the matter.

"Yes?"

He grimaced. "I may have amnesia, but I'm not blind. It's obvious she wants me to keep my hands to myself."

The doctor's mouth quivered for a moment. "And you don't want to...er...keep them to yourself?"

He thrust his few belongings into the plastic bag. "Not hardly," he said flatly. "I can accept that she's uncomfortable because of everything that's happened, but we're married and it's my baby. If everything is okay between us, why is it such an issue?"

Paige smiled. "Women are funny about things like this, Nick. Especially *pregnant* women. You know you're married, and so does she. But you don't remember her, and you act and say things in ways that aren't expected."

"I don't have the right words, or the right touches," he murmured, recalling his thoughts that first day when Emily had walked into the hospital room and he'd been filled with both pride and frustration. Not to mention lust. He stood and paced around the room. "Could it hurt Emily or the baby for us to be together?"

"Not unless there are some abnormal signs like bleeding or pain. Give her time," Paige advised. "Your memory will come back soon enough. Until then...get to know Emily again. Let her get to know you. You might learn some things you didn't know before."

"I keep thinking something is wrong," he muttered, sticking his fingers into the pockets of his jeans. "More than the amnesia."

"Oh, Nick." Paige shook her head. "You can't resume your life as though nothing happened. But you'll do fine. I've never seen two people who care so much about each other."

Nick nodded, hoping she was right—hoping she wasn't just being "the doctor" again, and feeding him the standard quotient of encouragement. He could court Emily again. It wouldn't kill him, though things were going to be pretty uncomfortable with all the cold showers he'd have to take.

He let the idea simmer, meanwhile objecting to the absurdity of being trundled out of the hospital in a wheelchair. It had been bad enough coming in on a stretcher. *The rules,* he thought darkly, feeling like an absolute idiot. But his irritation vanished when he saw Emily waiting for him at the entrance. Her hair shone in a golden halo about her face, and her long skirt and blouse were deliciously transparent in the sunlight.

Heaven.

Absolute heaven. He let himself relax.

"Hey, buddy. You look great," a male voice said from somewhere near. "And so does Emily, you lucky dog."

Nick didn't take his eyes from Emily, but he felt a flash of annoyance that another man was ogling his wife. Emily wasn't tall—the top of her head came only to his shoulder—but she was proportioned in all the right places. And she was pregnant with his baby. Perfection.

"She's beautiful," he agreed, glancing at the man who'd spoken to him. Some kind of law enforcement officer. Swell, he ought to be reminded that to "protect and serve" didn't include leering at someone else's wife.

"You don't know me, do you?" the officer asked.

Nick hesitated. Those type of questions were like land mines when you had amnesia. "Should I?"

The other man grinned, apparently unconcerned. "I'm Hank McAllister. Along with Emily's brother, Gabe, the three of us were the terror of Crockett in our high school days. Fortunately we mellowed. I even got respectable." He pointed to the badge on his uniform.

"Oh." Nick still didn't recognize the officer.

"Never mind." Hank slapped him on the shoulder. "We can talk about the old days some other time. I've got to get back on duty."

With a nod and sympathetic smile for Emily, Hank strode to his cruiser. Nick gritted his teeth. He didn't like anyone being so familiar with Emily. Maybe he didn't remember some things at the moment. But *he* was the husband.

"What was he doing here?"

Surprise at Nick's sharp tone widened Emily's eyes. "Hank's been a big help. I didn't have the car, so he took me home after the accident. He's taken a lot of—"

"He's too late."

"What?"

"You're already married."

Emily would have laughed if she hadn't been flabbergasted. He was jealous? Nick? "He's your friend, not mine. And there's never been anything like that with Hank."

"Keep it that way."

"You're being idiotic. Paige thought seeing him might jog your memory."

"Next time warn me. I don't like surprises."

"Since when?" Disgusted, she unlocked the passenger door of the Blazer for him, wishing she could kick Nick in the rear end. It might jog his memory, since he was acting like all his brains were down there, anyway.

Nick sighed as he climbed into the shiny blue four-by-four parked at the curb. He hadn't really disliked Hank McAllister—but he'd been unreasonably jealous because Hank knew more about his wife than he did. At least for the present.

Tight-lipped, Emily drove through Crockett. The community was tucked into a small inlet of the Puget Sound, with an attractive harbor and a tidy downtown shopping area. On the other side of town she drove up a quiet street and parked in the driveway of a house overlooking the harbor and inlet. Like the rest of Crockett, the house and neighborhood was neatly kept and profuse with flowers and trees.

"Is this where we live?"

Emily nodded, turning off the motor and sitting for a long moment with her fingers flexing about the steering wheel.

Nick took a deep breath and tried again. "Is it the house you grew up in?"

She cast a quick glance at him. "No. Mom and Dad

were still living in Crockett when I bought this place.''
She looked at the house, pride creeping into her tense
expression. ''It was a wreck, so I didn't have to pay very
much. You've been helping me fix it up and do some
remodeling.''

A frown of concentration creased his forehead. ''Of
course I've been helping, I'm your husband.''

A faint tinge of color brightened Emily's skin, and
she ducked her head as she opened the car door.
''Well...I bought it several years ago. Before we got
married.''

Nick got out and looked at the house. Not old enough
to be a Victorian, it was one of those solid, comfortable
homes built around 1920, with wide porches and big
picture windows. The kind of place you could fill with
a half-dozen kids. He'd even bet there was a tree swing
in the backyard.

''Dr. Wescott said I was working on the roof when I
fell.''

''Oh, yes. Around back.'' Emily fidgeted with her
wedding ring. ''There's a screened porch there, and it's
been leaking a lot.''

''I'll finish it as soon as possible.''

Emily threw back her head and glared at him. ''You'll
do nothing of the sort, Nicholas Carleton.''

He hid a grin. ''Why not?''

''Because I said so. Do you want to break your neck?
We'll get a proper roofer this time. I...I thought you
were dead when you fell.''

The faint quaver in her voice turned Nick's heart into
mush. Emily had to care about him, to be so worried.
''Easy, Angel,'' he murmured, sliding his arm around
her. God, she was wonderful, smelling of sunshine and

flowers and her uniquely feminine scent. "I'm not going to get hurt."

"That's right, because you're not getting on the roof again," she said, pulling away and stomping up the front steps.

Nick would have laughed, but he didn't want to upset Emily any more than necessary. His wife was soft and sentimental one minute, and feisty the next. But she had an inner core of sweetness that couldn't be disguised, no matter how determinedly she stuck out her chin and defied the world.

Inside, the house was cool and quiet, decorated with an artful simplicity that appealed to Nick's senses. Cut wildflowers rested in a pottery pitcher on the mantel. Comfortable, modern furniture blended with a few antiques. A breeze lifted lace curtains at the windows, and the scent of lemon wafted through the air to mingle with homey smells of spice and yeast and freshly cut grass from a neighbor's yard.

Though he felt like an intruder, he strolled from room to room, opening a drawer or closet and peering inside.

"Looking for something?" Emily looked up at him warily as he wandered into the master bedroom on the second floor. She tossed her shoes into the closet and stood there, biting her lip and shifting her bare feet.

"Our room?" he asked unnecessarily.

"Uh-huh."

His gaze followed her restless movements as she turned the plain gold wedding band around on her finger. He lifted her hand and kissed the ring, letting his lips linger for a moment, intrigued by the contrast of smooth metal and warm skin. "Why didn't I get you a diamond?" he murmured.

"Oh...I don't like fancy rings. They get in the way,

and I'd worry about losing it or something.'' She tried to pull away without quite meeting his gaze.

"Don't be nervous," he whispered.

"I should be saying that to you."

"Why should I be nervous?" Nick gathered Emily against him, tucking her head beneath his chin. "Because I have amnesia?" He felt her shrug. "Am I so different now, than before?"

"It's not that simple. Look, maybe you should rest. I'll go downstairs and leave you alone."

Nick tipped Emily's face up and gazed into her eyes. "You're my wife," he said slowly and distinctly. "I don't know what happened in the past, but I know what I want now."

"Sex," she said flatly.

Ouch.

But it was his own fault, since he'd taken every opportunity to touch her since the first moment he'd seen her. Sure, sex was part of what he wanted, but he also wanted his life back. The life where Emily laughed with him, fought with him, loved him...trusted him. *All* of it.

"What's wrong with sex?" he asked, stalling for time.

Her gaze flickered. "Nothing. But I told you, it's uncomfortable with the baby coming. Just give me some time."

"How much time?" he whispered, bending so close their breath mingled.

"I...I don't know."

"Mmm." Nick traced the piping on the neckline of Emily's eyelet blouse and sensed her breathing quicken. He flicked open the top button. Desire and reluctance warred in her deep blue eyes. The desire he'd aroused and the reluctance he'd sensed in her from the beginning.

What he was doing wasn't fair. But he didn't want to be fair, he wanted Emily.

Taking the edge of the fabric between his fingers he shook his head. "This stuff is awfully thin. Did you realize it's transparent with the light behind you?"

Emily blinked. She wanted to be outraged, but her blood was pumping so hard she couldn't even think. "I...Nick...."

The second button went.

"I could see everything in the sunlight."

"I'm getting fat," Emily muttered.

He caressed her rounded belly. "You're beautiful. I only want you more, knowing my baby is growing inside you."

The third and fourth button opened.

"And your breasts..." Nick nudged the blouse open. "They're such a lovely shape. I could see them, all outlined with light and shadow."

Emily's knees shook, and with an easy, fluid motion he swept them both to the bed. She knew her breasts were drawn tight and aching, the nipples so sensitive that she could feel every pulse, every warm breath across them. It didn't seem real—as though it wasn't really Nick making her feel these things.

But it *was* Nick, and she had to stop him before their friendship was destroyed.

"Nick...we can't—"

"You're like a wonderful dream," he murmured, stopping her protest. Putting one arm under her neck he kissed her hard, arching her head into the pillows. Tasting...testing, teasing her with a practiced skill. It was the skill that bothered her most, but she had trouble getting her muddled brain to pay attention.

Endless moments later he released her, sliding down

her body, imprinting a heated trail of kisses. But it wasn't until his palm closed over her right breast that she realized he'd somehow unhooked her bra and gotten it off her.

"How did you do that?" she gasped, attempting to sit up.

In the process of kissing her belly button, Nick laughed. "I don't know. Seems to have come naturally."

Natural talent. She might have known. It must be one of those abilities his dissociative amnesia hadn't erased. Emily held out her hand and tried to frown. "Where is it?"

"Where's what?"

"Very funny. Give me my bra."

"Here," said Nick, but instead of dropping it into her fingers he clasped their hands together and drew her arm over her head. As a result she got another soul-searing kiss and her thoughts turned mushy again.

Definitely mushy.

Emily threaded the fingers of her free hand through Nick's hair, intending to pull him away. Yet she couldn't, at least not yet. *This can't be happening.* Twisting, she drew her leg up against his hip, a new, hot pressure spinning through her abdomen. It was so overwhelming, this feeling.

"Nick..." she breathed between the gliding forays of his tongue. No longer fighting, just accepting the sensuous spell he'd cast over them both.

Nick groaned. He'd taken things too far. Emily might be willing to make love with him at the moment, but he'd sensed she'd regret it later. And then she'd want to crown him.

At the same time, she'd probably want to kill him for stopping.

"You're right," he said, reluctantly pulling away. "This isn't the time."

"What?" Disbelief, mixed with frustrated fury, darkened her eyes.

"I'd better take a shower." *A cold shower.* He'd need a glacier to cool him down at this point.

"Nick?"

He wanted to howl when he twisted away, practically running for the door. As he closed it behind him he heard a muffled shriek, then the distinctive sound of shattering glass.

Nick leaned against the wall and breathed hard. She must have thrown the water glass he'd seen on the bedside table. Then again, she might have just dropped it.

"Angel," he called, opening the door, "don't get up, you've got bare feet. I'll get the broom and dustpan. Uh...where do we keep them?"

Chapter Four

Emily bent over her accounting sheets from the shop and tried to concentrate. It wasn't easy. An hour later her body still throbbed from the fever pitch Nick had aroused.

Don't think about it.

Huh, she hadn't been able to think about anything else. Her business would be ruined by the time Nick got his memory back. Few things could compete with an earthquake, and that's what it felt like when he kissed her.

Think about the baby.

Emily chewed on the end of her pencil and stared into space. She'd always wanted children, and every day she'd been inundated with reminders. Babies. Pregnant women. Kids in pigtails and jumpers and overalls. A never-ending parade of family life through her little clothing shop. *Constantly.*

So, she had decided to take matters into her own hands. It might be unusual to have a baby by artificial insemination, but it had seemed logical at the time. *That* was before Nick fell off the roof. *That* was before he'd kissed her and short-circuited every logical cell in her body.

"Mooorow."

"Get off the table, GeeZee," she mumbled. She pushed at the black-and-white cat, who casually plonked himself down on top of her work as though he'd been invited. He purred as she absently scratched beneath his chin.

"What're you doing?" Nick asked, surprising her.

Emily put a hand on her throat, fighting the instant awareness in her body. Blast Nick. It was bad enough pretending they had a normal marriage, why did he have to make her feel so...so *wanton.* She'd never felt anything so powerful in her life. Not with Kevin, not with any man. Over the years she'd accepted the fact she wasn't passionate. She liked the preliminaries, but there weren't many fireworks.

Now she'd had an attack of lust for the last man she should ever go to bed with...her best friend.

And husband, a voice whispered inside her head.

Emily decided to ignore the voice...it was safer that way. "I...uh...bought my parents' business in Crockett a couple of years ago. We sell kids' clothing and maternity outfits," she explained, tugging a ledger from beneath GeeZee. "I had some paperwork to go over."

"May I help?"

She wanted to suggest he could help by leaving, but decided it wouldn't sound very "wifely."

"It's boring stuff. Look around the house," she suggested instead. "It might help you remember."

"I've already looked at the house," Nick said, exasperated. "It's a great house, an incredible house. It's perfect for us to raise a bunch of kids in—but you're my wife, and I want to spend time with you. Not a damn house.''

''You never—''

''Sorry,'' he said, holding up his hand in a peaceful gesture. ''I know, I shouldn't have cursed. You don't like it in front of the baby. *Our* baby.''

Emily glared. ''You *never liked this house.* You said I was foolish to buy it.''

He rested his palms on the table and bent forward until they were nose to nose. ''Let's set some ground rules,'' he growled. ''I won't lie to you. And you don't bring up any old arguments I can't possibly defend myself over. We can fight when I get my memory back.''

''But you said—''

''I don't care what I said. I'm wild about the house. Absolutely crazy. But I'd be a whole lot crazier about the place if we'd spent the past hour making love in that bed upstairs.''

She swallowed and felt heat creeping up her body. Only it wasn't embarrassment, it was the memory of Nick's weight on top of her, and the tingling, itching need he'd built, but hadn't eased.

''You were the one who stopped,'' she whispered, before she could think better of it.

Nick slumped into a chair. ''Don't remind me. I was trying to be noble and sensitive.''

Emily rubbed her forehead, too confused to understand herself, much less Nick. It was the pregnancy. *That* was the answer. She'd read about it in one of her books. Sometimes women became more…aroused, because of the increased blood flow in the abdomen.

She didn't really want to sleep with Nick—her buddy.

It was just a biological response to childbearing. A dose of prenatally induced libido. Yeah, that sounded good.

Just then Nick smiled at her, little laugh lines crinkling the corner of his eyes.

Or maybe not.

"You could look at some photo albums," she suggested breathlessly. "I have family books, and there are some you kept before we...uh...got married."

"I can do that later." He reached over to pet GeeZee, who promptly opened his mouth and spat at him. A small frown appeared on Nick's face. "Er...kitty?"

GeeZee spat again and switched his tail.

"He acts like I'm a total stranger," Nick said, puzzled by the feline's odd reaction.

Emily's eyes widened. "GeeZee, be nice. What's wrong with you?"

Quite deliberately the feline rose to his feet, turned his back and jumped from the table. A loud thud resounded through the air, the result of twenty-four pounds of cat hitting a hardwood floor—GeeZee had never suffered from a lack of appetite.

A small, twinging pain went through Nick's head and he rubbed his temples. *Another mystery.* But at least Emily seemed genuinely puzzled, as well. "I think I've been snubbed," he muttered.

"He's never acted like that before." Emily shook her head. "Cats are strange, and you really startled him when you fell off the roof—maybe he's still mad about that. They hate to lose their dignity."

"Hey," Nick said, forcing a cheerful note into the word. "I think GeeZee just realizes I'm not myself. I've been thinking a lot about this stuff. I probably didn't touch him right."

Emily didn't say anything, and he sighed.

"Angel?" He brushed the side of her face, and her gaze focused on him. "I seem different to you, too. That's part of the problem, isn't it?"

She blinked. "There isn't a problem."

"Right, and I'm the Prince of Wales."

"How would you know? Your highness," she retorted.

Nick chuckled as he pulled Emily into his lap. "You've made your point." He kissed the end of her nose. "Can you take some time off from work? Maybe we could go sailing."

"Sailing?" Emily wiggled upright using his chest for ballast. She searched Nick's face. Did he remember something? "Why sailing?"

"It sounds like fun, and there's a picture of us on a boat. Right over there."

He pointed to a framed photo of them on Nick's boat, *The Lazy Skipper.* Emily thought about the day they'd taken it, laughing at the absurdity of setting a timer on a rolling deck in the middle of Puget Sound. They'd really laughed when the shot turned out great.

"Actually, it isn't a sailboat," she murmured. "It's thirty-two feet of fiberglass and power."

"Power?"

"You prefer speed," she said, sliding from his lap and straightening her clothing. "But you opted for a little speed and a lot of luxury. You've always been restless. You like to travel and try different things. Different food, different everything." She grinned. "You couldn't wait to get out of Crockett."

"When did I change my mind?"

"What?"

"I'm living in Crockett now. When did I change my mind about it?"

Emily's skin went cold. Blast. That's what happened when you got too confident and spoke without thinking. She'd told more lies in the past couple of days than she'd told in her entire life.

Well...mostly she'd just allowed Nick to believe what he wanted to believe—which was interesting, because Nick had never wanted marriage or babies. He'd only interfered with her plan because he was conservative and overprotective when it came to the woman he thought of as family.

"In a way," she said carefully, "you didn't change. You still travel a lot for your work. And you're always making me eat strange things. No matter how hard I try, I hate *calimari* and *escargots,* but you love that kind of stuff."

"Sorry about that." Nick dropped a kissed on her cheek, and his hand went unerringly to her stomach, rubbing carefully. The warmth penetrated the thin cotton of her dress, and she bit back a moan of both guilt and pleasure. It would have been wonderful if he really felt so close, excited and wanting the baby.

"It...it's not so bad," she managed to say.

"No. I shouldn't make you do anything you don't want. Especially now."

He sounded sincere and loving, so protective of both her and the baby that her heart turned over. Emily leaned into him, remembering the times she'd gotten apprehensive about becoming a single mother and taking such a big step in her life. She couldn't discuss it with her family, they would have just given her a smug "We told you so." And she hadn't been able to talk about her fears with Nick—it wouldn't have been fair after all he'd done.

"I thought you wanted to go boating," she said, eas-

ing from the comforting embrace. She couldn't become
dependent on Nick. Once his memory came back, she'd
be lucky if he ever spoke to her again. Even the prospect
of getting seasick was better than answering uncomfortable questions.

"Is it that simple?"

"It is when you own the boat. She's moored down in
the harbor."

At his look of pleasure, Emily smiled. "I'll pack a
picnic lunch, then we'll go down to the dock so I can
introduce you to your *other* baby."

This is the life, Nick decided, relaxing in the helm
seat as they glided along the rugged shore of the Puget
Sound. It felt wonderful to be out with Emily, cruising
the water and enjoying the sunshine. But he wasn't interested in the speed and power she'd said he loved,
rather in the privacy and freedom afforded by the boat.

He'd instinctively known how to handle the thirty-
two-foot vessel, guiding it easily out of Crockett Harbor.
Various people had waved a greeting at them, and he'd
waved right back, with Emily whispering their names in
his ear.

Amnesia was an awfully funny thing. He could remember Coast Guard signals and marine law, yet he
couldn't recall the names of his friends.

"Shall we anchor for a while?" he asked, glancing at
Emily. He'd kept a close watch on her, concerned about
the faint pallor of her skin and the shadows beneath her
eyes.

"Sure."

Nick turned the boat into a quiet, shaded cove. He
didn't want Emily getting sunburned—she had refused
to wear any sunscreen protection, fearful of hurting the

baby. He hadn't argued because he didn't know if the chemical *could* do harm, even applied externally.

Emily shifted her feet as he moored *The Lazy Skipper*. "Would you like to eat now, or later?" she asked.

"Later, I guess, unless you're hungry. You're eating for two, after all." He motioned to her rounded tummy.

"I'm fine," she assured him, rolling her eyes. "I drank a glass of milk before we left the house. Honestly, you fuss too much. I'm perfectly capable of getting enough nutrition without any nagging."

"I don't—" Nick let his protest fade at her annoyed expression. "Okay. Let's relax for a while," he said, opening a couple of deck chairs on the stern. "Then we'll eat."

They stretched out in the comfortable seats, and though Nick closed his eyes, he was aware of the slightest movement Emily made. Her breathing gradually became slow and rhythmic, lulled by the restful rocking of the boat. When he was certain she was asleep, he turned on his side to watch her.

It was the first time he'd been able to look at his wife without distraction. She was so beautiful it took his breath away.

My wife.

The words settled into his heart and made a satisfying impression.

I'm going to be a father.

Those words were equally satisfying. He could easily imagine falling in love with Emily. What surprised him was the length of time it had taken them to get together—she was thirty-three, and he was thirty-six. They'd only been married for a few months, but they'd known each other since childhood.

Nick rubbed his face and tried to ease the knot of

worry in his gut. Why had they waited so long? Why did GeeZee treat him like a stranger? More and more questions kept getting raised, with no apparent answers. He could understand the shadows beneath Emily's eyes. They could be explained by worry. But what about the rest?

Damnation.

He flipped open the ice chest and grabbed a soft drink from the picnic she'd packed for them. A light wind from the north ruffled the waters of the cove. It was tranquil, unlike the clamoring questions inside his head.

Yet what was he tearing himself up about? Judging by the expensive boat they owned, he had a successful career. He had a nice home, a beautiful wife and a baby on the way. According to Emily, there was even a Porsche 911 in the garage next to the house. Overall his life looked pretty nice, so why was he picking everything apart with futile concerns?

After almost an hour, Emily opened her eyes and yawned, disturbed by the backwash of several jet boats speeding past the opening of the cove. "It's getting busy out there," she murmured. Small beads of perspiration dampened her forehead and he leaned forward.

"Are you...uh, feeling okay, Angel?"

She swallowed cautiously. "So-so. I brought some saltine crackers, just in case my stomach couldn't decide if it was morning or afternoon."

"Crackers?"

Emily shook her head and gave him a wry smile. "Honestly, Nick, you don't know anything. Saltines help morning sickness. And don't blame amnesia, you've never liked dealing with 'feminine' stuff."

A brief scowl tightened his face. At the moment, Emily had an unfair advantage in their relationship. "I don't care about what I did or didn't do before. You're having my baby and I want to help. I saw some books about childbirth at the house, I'll read them as soon as possible.''

Emily flushed. If she wasn't careful, she'd start sounding like a shrew. "Sorry," she mumbled. "Actually, I learned a lot about being pregnant from working at the store.''

Nick took a deep breath, visibly calming himself. "You sell maternity and children's clothing, right?''

She nodded. Nick seemed to remember everything she told him, even the smallest detail of their lives. "It's called Mom and Kid's Stuff. We're very successful. We get women from all over the area because we carry a good selection of business maternity wear.''

He gave her an encouraging nod and she relaxed. It was nice, being out on the boat, even though her stomach kept churning. Nick had been working out of the country for more than a month, so they hadn't used it recently.

"Don't other stores carry business wear?'' he asked.

"Sure, but most designers seem to think women revert to childhood when they're having a baby," Emily murmured. "Big bows, puff sleeves, and cutesy appliqués. They don't realize that pregnant women still want to feel sexy and attractive—even though we look like legs attached to a beach ball.''

From the corner of her eye she saw Nick sit up. "You have to be kidding," he said.

"No, you should see some of this stuff. It's godawful. Frills and bows. Childish prints. Big flannel nightgowns with stand-up collars at the neck and enough fabric to cover the King Dome roof.''

"That's not what I meant.'' Nick lifted her hand and

kissed the back of it. She shivered, though not from cold. "You're beautiful pregnant. It makes me feel very... lively, knowing you're carrying my child."

"Lively?" Emily turned her head and really looked at him. Awareness crept up her body. Nick's worn jeans did little to disguise what he meant by *lively*. "Never mind," she mumbled. Since waking up without his memory, he seemed to think it was his single most important duty to get her into bed.

If she'd been a normal wife she might have enjoyed his determined seduction. Yet she couldn't forget how mortified they would be when Nick got his memory back and realized he'd wanted to make love to the woman he'd always called "kid."

, Mortified? Right. He'd probably be furious. Or else he'd laugh his head off, which might be worse.

The tip of his tongue flicked her skin and she squirmed in her chair. *Damn him.* Here she was, with her queasy stomach sticking up in the air, and he was making her feel sexy and wanted and utterly desirable. The look in Nick's eyes was so incredible. Gentle, loving, concerned...with flickers of passion banked hot and deep. It was a new, unfamiliar side of him...a side she'd never expected to see.

"Nick," she whispered helplessly, melting as he knelt beside her.

His hand stroked gently over her stomach, and she realized it wasn't sticking up in the air as much as she'd thought. It was just a nice little mound, enough for Nick to cup his hand over. And her breasts...they were tight and achy, and she wanted to feel his mouth, suckling, drawing her in....

The baby. He's just thinking about the baby.

He's got amnesia.

He's not responsible. Remember that. He's playing some kind of role because he wants to believe his life is getting back to normal.

Emily wanted to murder the persistent voice—the voice that kept reminding her there were a thousand logical reasons Nick *thought* he wanted her, none of which *really* had anything to do with her. Not really.

God, that was depressing.

"You're still tired," Nick murmured, his free hand tracing the downward curve of her mouth. "I know how difficult this has been."

She shrugged without looking up. "Like I said, I may be little, but I'm—"

"Tough," he finished for her. "You're also my wife and you're pregnant with my baby. I have the right to be concerned, don't I?" With a frustrated motion he raked his fingers through his hair and leaned against the side of the boat.

Emily closed her eyes. She didn't want to see Nick sitting there, looking sexy and wonderful. Cripes, it wasn't like he was wearing a tuxedo or anything. He was wearing a chambray work shirt and jeans. Worn-out jeans. The same jeans she'd washed and mended numerous times.

Good.

She needed to think about something safe, and laundry qualified. Like that time a huge, exotic beetle had stowed away in his duffel bag when he'd come back from Brazil...Emily grimaced at the memory. Nick had laughed himself silly when he'd found her on top of the washing machine—she still wasn't sure if he'd planned the whole thing as a joke.

"What are you glaring about?"

Emily caught her bottom lip between her teeth and bit

hard. "I was thinking about the laundry," she said honestly. "You bring some weird stuff back from all those other countries. You got home a few days ago, and I haven't touched the latest batch yet. I may have it fumigated first."

Nick watched her intently and she shifted, uncomfortable with the close regard. What did he want?

An image flashed into her mind of two people intertwined on a bed.

Oh.

Right.

That's what he wanted. A little horizontal activity with his "wife."

"How come *The Lazy Skipper?*" Nick asked after a long minute.

"Well...it's a private joke." She smiled. "When you traded in the ski boat, I teased you about getting lazy. You opted for all kind of extras that would make this one easier to maintain. But she's still a lot of work."

"I see. Do we use her often?"

"Whenever you're home."

Two more boats raced past the mouth of the cove and *The Lazy Skipper* rolled with the backwash, disturbing Emily's already upset stomach. She gulped, nausea pushing other thoughts from her mind. Standing, she lurched to the side, almost falling into the water in her haste.

"Whoa." Nick caught her knees, then worked his grasp up her body as her stomach revenged itself. "It's all right," he murmured.

All right?

If Emily hadn't been so miserable, she would have kicked him. While it was totally illogical, she wanted to scream that she was sick because of *his* baby, and *his* boat, and *his* stupid amnesia. But she couldn't, because it also felt safe and good to have him holding her, with one hand supporting her forehead, and his other arm around her waist.

When the dry spasms eased, Nick put her back in the deck chair. He disappeared into the galley for a moment and returned with a wet cloth. "I'm sorry. It's my fault," he murmured, gently wiping her face. "It was selfish to go boating when you feel this way. I just thought..." He shrugged and drew the cloth down her throat.

Emily managed to lift a questioning eyebrow at him. "Thought what?"

"I thought it would be a chance for us to get to know each other."

She shivered. "Why worry about that? You're going to remember everything. A day or two, that's all. And the boat was a good idea. Paige said you should do familiar things, because it would help you get your memory back."

Nick frowned thoughtfully. He wiped the inside of Emily's wrists. She seemed so delicate and fragile, no matter how tough and independent she tried to act. Maybe she didn't trust him to take care of her. "We have to accept the possibility I might never remember," he said slowly.

"Don't say that!" Emily yelped. Alarm widened her blue eyes. "You'll get your memory back, Nick. You have to!"

"Hey, take it easy, Angel," he soothed. "One day at a time, remember?"

"One day at a— That's not what we were talking about when you said..." Her voice trailed off, and a hint of color returned to her face.

Nick kissed the palm of her hand. The proviso about

"one day at a time" referred to their bedroom status.
But he wasn't above distracting Emily by any means
available. "I'm sorry about pushing. I guess you really
meant that part about wanting to wait because of the
baby."

"What...what did you think I meant?" Absently, she
turned her wedding ring around on her finger.

"I don't know." He gave her a wry smile. "I worry
that you don't want to be intimate for other reasons.
Like...maybe because we're having marital problems."
Nick didn't quite make his statement a question, but
there was an inquiring note to the last word.

"We aren't having marital problems," she said
firmly.

Nick nodded. He wasn't convinced, but he didn't want
to push the matter. Hell, Emily was pregnant. She could
be affected by all kinds of things. Even the happiest
couple must go through adjustments with their first baby.

"Let's go back," he said. "I don't want you getting
sick again."

Emily just nodded.

By the time they reached the house, Emily's head
ached from pretending everything was okay. Nick fussed
about that a lot. She supposed he had reason, because
everything *wasn't* okay—at least not the okay he
wanted.

It'll be fine. When he remembers.

When he remembers.... For the past few days she'd
been repeating those words like a mantra. But she
couldn't escape a growing fear that nothing she did
would be enough, and that nothing would ever be the
same between them.

How could they forget the sensual kisses? The intimate touches and words? Or would Nick just crack a

joke about it and go on with his carefree life? And how could she bear it if he did?

Uh-oh.

Emily gulped. She wasn't thinking too clearly. Of course she wanted things to be normal again. She wanted the same old Nick. The same old relationship. Romance was too much work, and in a few months she'd have her hands full with the baby, anyhow.

"Angel? You're awfully quiet. Do you need to lie down?" Nick asked as he closed the heavy front door.

"Oh…no. I slept on the boat, remember?" Emily smoothed her hands over her skirt self-consciously. She wasn't accustomed to Nick watching her so closely, seeing every nuance of expression. It made her feel strange.

"The nausea?"

"Much better." She tried to take the ice chest he carried, but Nick shook his head and carried their still-uneaten lunch to the kitchen for her. Emily sighed and followed. "I'm sorry I spoiled your first day home."

He looked at her, genuine surprise in his eyes. "You didn't spoil anything. You're pregnant. I should have realized the boat was a bad idea. I'm the one who should apologize."

"But—"

"No." Nick dropped a light kiss on her forehead. "It's fine. Let's eat that picnic, then I'll get to work on the nursery."

Emily blinked, not knowing what to think. How did he know about the nursery she'd planned? Did it mean his memory was coming back? "The…uh, nursery?"

"Next to our bedroom, right?"

She nodded.

Nick pulled the food from the chest. "I saw the paint

cans and some boxes with a crib and stuff when I explored the house. I assumed it was for the baby."

"Yes...but you should take it easy for a couple of days," she murmured. "You just got out of the hospital. We can take care of it later. It's a while before the baby gets here."

"Dr. Wescott said I could resume my normal activities," Nick said amiably, though his eyes glinted. "That's what I intend to do. I'm feeling restless. The activity will help."

He turned a chair around and straddled it—the gesture sending tremors through Emily because he often sat like that. Once, he had told her about his first foster home—about the arguing and name-calling during mealtimes. Almost three decades separated child and man from the ugly images, but he still put the barrier of a chair between him and the table.

Even with amnesia.

Nick smiled and Emily pushed the melancholy thought away. "Okay. I hope you like the colors—yellow with white trim work. I want it to be bright and sunny."

"Sounds nice."

In short order the sandwiches, macaroni salad and assorted condiments disappeared down his throat. Emily managed to drink another glass of milk and nibbled some crackers—she wasn't eager to stress her abused stomach. With any luck this late-blooming, all-day-morning sickness would vanish as quickly as it had arrived.

She could only hope.

After eating they went upstairs, only to start another argument—this time about Emily doing any painting.

"Absolutely not," Nick declared. He backed her into

the hallway. "You aren't straining yourself, and that's that."

"You're being silly."

"I'm being sensible. The fumes could hurt you and the baby, not to mention the lifting and stretching. Besides, you've been upset because of my accident. We're not taking any chances."

Emily held on to her temper...barely. "Exercise is good for me. And the paint is that new, nontoxic, no-fume variety. I could practically drink the stuff."

"Well, you're not drinking it, and you're not doing any painting. You can sit out here and give me directions. That's what you get. Take it, or leave it."

Her mouth dropped open for a minute, then she snapped it shut. Of all the nerve! Take it or leave it? He couldn't order her around. This was *her* house, even if she had to pretend it belonged to them both.

"Look—"

"No." He crossed his arms, looking as immovable as a mountain.

"Be reasonable." Emily took a couple of deep breaths. "I could have easily finished the redecorating while you were out of the country."

"It's a good thing you didn't." Nick rolled up his sleeves and calmly began organizing the room, but the moment she put one foot across the doorway he cast her a fierce glare. "I mean it, Angel. Stay out."

She rolled her eyes. Impossible. Utterly impossible. "This is nuts. You wouldn't have minded before you got amnesia. I always planned to do the nursery myself, and you didn't have any objections. You said you'd help, but you knew I'd be doing most of it."

He dropped the tarp he was spreading across the floor and went to her. "I object now. And frankly, I don't care what I did or said before. It's my responsibility to take care of you and the baby, and that's what I'm going to do."

"Nick! This is the twentieth century, not the twelfth. I can take care of myself."

"Please, Angel," Nick murmured. "Don't fight me on this."

He cupped her face between his fingers, and she was suddenly aware of how big Nick was, and how small she felt in comparison. No wonder he perceived her as helpless. He was taller, more powerful and could do things with one hand it would take all her strength to accomplish.

Putting her hands over his wrists, Emily tried to smile. "I don't give up easily."

"No kidding." An instant later he kissed her, his warmth and energy flowing over her like liquid sunlight. And when he stepped away she felt strangely bereft.

Get hold of yourself, she ordered.

Nick-the-husband would soon be Nick-the-pal again, and she'd be on her own. When his memory did return, her only hope lay in convincing him she was a great actress, with a great sense of humor, who'd played along knowing they'd both laugh about it in the end.

His big hand cupped her stomach, rubbing gently. "You take care of junior. I'll get a comfortable chair for you to sit in," he whispered.

Emily blinked. Five minutes later she was seated with her feet up, watching Nick stir paint and wondering how he'd gotten her to just watch. It defied the imagination.

It had to be the kiss. Her brain was scrambled.

Emily tapped her fingers on the chair arm and thought. So she was pregnant. That didn't make her incapable. Pregnant women could do normal things like painting

and putting up decorations. She didn't have to be treated
like a piece of fragile porcelain.

Still...it was kind of nice, in a dumb sort of way.
Rather like a trip to Disneyland, where you pretend
you're still a kid or a princess, or scared of a haunted
house with more high-tech gadgetry than NASA. Of
course...there was that time a Disney employee had
dressed up in a suit of armor and lunged at Nick unexpectedly. She'd really shrieked over that stunt.

Nick had just laughed. She didn't think anything
scared the bozo.

"You missed a spot," she called out.

He grinned at her. An endearing bozo, she had to admit. With better pecs than most of the hunks in the mov-
ies. And, except for the occasions when his male pre-
cepts got in the way, he wasn't that dumb.

"You don't appreciate my style," Nick said. He
wiped a drip of paint from his forehead.

Emily sighed and decided to relax. Her pregnancy had
already caused some changes in balance and posture.
Getting in and out of the Blazer wasn't nearly as easy,
and she thought twice about jumping on a chair to
change a lightbulb. She might as well let Nick enjoy
being the "man," since he was determined to do it, anyway.

"Do you want any wallpaper?" he asked after a com-
panionable silence.

She yawned. "I have some decorative *ABC* strips.
You know, the kind with animals. It's really cute."

He nodded and kept working, so she put her head
back, listening to the swish of wet paint being efficiently
applied. Nick moved the roller up and down in broad,
even strokes, his shirt drawn taut against his muscles. It

wouldn't take long for the little room to become a beautiful nursery.

"Tell me how we fell in love," he said as he moved to the far wall.

Swell. Emily slumped deeper in her chair. Just when you got comfortable because things were going well, everything fell apart. She grimaced at Nick's back.

"Angel?"

The nickname tugged at her heart. When he called her *Angel* she felt like the most special woman in the world. She would miss that feeling when she got the real Nick back.

"I'm not sure what to say," she said, stalling. "We've known each other forever."

"But there must have been a point we decided we were in love."

"Well...it kind of crept up on us. We were friends and spent a lot of time together. We even went on joint vacations. All kinds of stuff."

GeeZee strolled down the hall and "merrowed" loudly. Emily scratched his ears and prayed Nick wouldn't keeping asking questions she couldn't answer. She was definitely going to work in the morning. If she wasn't around, he couldn't ask.

"What took so long?" he queried, sounding casual. "If we were that close, we should have fallen in love sooner."

Emily looked at her "husband's" back a second time and scowled. Maybe he sounded casual, but she had the impression he was fiercely interested in the answer.

"I don't know," she said. "We were in different points in our lives. But we're together now. That's what's important, right?"

Nick turned his head and smiled—a searing, electric

smile that sent sensual shivers to her toes and back. "Yes."

Emily fanned herself again, for much different reasons than summer heat.

Drat those pregnancy hormones.

Just because Nick turned out to be the biggest, baddest, sexiest, most intense man to ever kiss her, she didn't have to give in to the impulse.

Sex was temporary.

Friendship was forever.

If he didn't have amnesia, she'd never be thinking of him in this way. Of course, mutual friends had often speculated about their relationship—sometimes none too subtly. But she and Nick had just laughed and gone on their own special way.

GeeZee leaped into her lap and settled himself in her arms. He purred contentedly, but kept a suspicious eye on Nick. Emily tapped his nose. She couldn't understand why GeeZee had suddenly decided he didn't like Nick. It didn't make any sense.

"He's too heavy," Nick said, glancing at the feline. "He should be on diet food."

"Do *you* want to explain that to him?"

As though making a point, GeeZee flexed one paw into an enormous hook.

"I guess not."

Nick completed the last wall and went to the bathroom to rinse the roller and paintbrush. Emily leaned forward, noting how much lighter the room seemed with the pale yellow color washing the walls and ceiling.

"Nice job," she called.

"I aim to please." He dropped a kiss on her head and went back into the room, purposefully opening the box containing the crib. "Don't worry," he said, "I'll cover everything with the tarp when I do the trim work."

Emily nodded, a little nonplussed. The real Nick was a big help. In fact, he insisted on helping and seemed hurt if she checked into other options. But he normally caused a project to lag behind where she wanted it to be, unless the project happened to be an emergency. She'd learned to propose a new project, then he'd finish her original one more quickly.

"Are you trying to impress me?" she asked.

"Would it work?"

"Gee, I don't know. That depends."

"Do I really have to impress you?" Nick assumed a hopeful expression. "After all, we're already married."

The corner of Emily's mouth twitched. "Smooth talker."

For the remainder of the afternoon and evening they kept things on a light, playful note. Nick didn't ask any more uncomfortable questions, and Emily truly relaxed for the first time since she'd seen him fly off the roof.

It wasn't until after she'd bathed and dressed for bed that the next dilemma loomed. Guiltily, she pulled sheets from the linen closet. She'd make up the spare bed Nick used when he visited. With any luck she'd be done before he was out of the shower.

The bathroom door opened. "What are you doing?"

Emily froze in mid-step. "I thought I'd sleep in the guest room tonight."

"No." The word wasn't angry, just firm and inflexible.

Plastering a smile on her face, she turned. "I'm awfully restless with the baby. You wouldn't get any sleep."

"I don't care."

Nick leaned one arm against the doorjamb, wearing nothing but a towel around his hips, his broad shoulders silhouetted in the soft light. He looked...overwhelmingly male. Emily clutched the sheets against her breasts. She couldn't very well argue that fumes from the new paint in the nursery bothered her, not after claiming it was nontoxic and fume free.

"I...I really think you'd be more comfortable sleeping alone."

"No."

The towel around Nick's hips shifted, and without haste he fastened it more securely. Emily hugged the sheets tighter, wondering how the air had gotten so stuffy all of a sudden. It wasn't as if she'd never seen Nick almost naked. They often went swimming together, and men's swim trunks left little to the imagination.

But that towel...

Get a grip.

Good advice. She was a mature woman—a mature *pregnant* woman. She didn't have to act like a neophyte teenager. She took a deep breath and calmly explained the various reasons she ought to sleep in a different bed.

With equal calm, Nick rejected the reasons. He was implacable, in a way she'd never seen him. He finally took the sheets from her arms and stuffed them back into the linen closet. Gently propelling her into the master bedroom, he gave her a kiss.

"I'll be in shortly. Will it keep you awake if I read for a while?"

Emily shook her head, confused by the odd blend of relief and disappointment flooding through her. If Nick wanted to read, he probably didn't have any plans to seduce her.

Because he seemed to be waiting, she shrugged out of her robe and slipped beneath the comforter. She was tired, and with any luck she could be asleep before Nick got back...or she could just pretend to be sleep.

Whatever it took.

Chapter Five

The house was quiet, the nighttime silence broken only
by the faint sound of paper crackling as Nick turned the
pages of a book on childbirth. His brow wrinkled in
concentration as he read. Amnesia or not, he was certain
the information was new to him.

He'd hoped to have flashes of "sure, I knew that."
Yet Emily seemed to be right about his ignorance.

You've never liked dealing with feminine stuff.

Contempt for his former self crawled across Nick's
skin. No wonder she acted as though she was all alone,
just her and the baby. And why shouldn't she feel that
way? Apparently he traveled extensively for his work,
so he didn't have a high profile as a husband and expectant father. Maybe it was a miracle Emily had married him at all.

Emily. Sweet, lively Emily.

She lay next to him on the mattress, breathing quietly,
one arm flung out in sleep. His eyes warmed with silent
appreciation. She wore a midnight blue satin nightgown

that clung to every curve of her body. He'd almost swallowed his tongue when he'd seen her in it.

A faint smile creased his mouth as he recalled her earnest arguments about using different bedrooms.

He'd refused, of course.

Whatever mistakes they might have made in the past, he didn't intend to make them worse. Married people slept together. Period. Separate beds would just put distance between them.

I'll disturb you if I get sick, she'd argued.

Hellfire. Why shouldn't she disturb him? She was pregnant with his child.

He looked back at the book. According to the experts, a woman could be particularly responsive during pregnancy, or her sex drive might be nonexistent. Either condition was normal, depending on the individual. The nonexistent part could be caused by different things— like physical discomfort or concerns about hurting the baby.

Nick glanced at Emily again. She worried about the baby; he knew that already. As for responding to him...well, she'd been pretty responsive that afternoon.

Still, he didn't need a book *or* his memory to know a pregnant woman could be unpredictable. Somewhere in the back of his mind he heard someone saying, *You just can't believe what they'll do or say!*

So far, that anonymous "someone" was right. Which meant he'd have to be extra understanding. Extra patient. Extra supportive. Extra *everything*. Most likely Emily had been acting strangely before his accident.

Probably.

He let out a quiet sigh as he put the book on the bedside table. A cool night breeze flowed through an open window—Emily said she couldn't sleep without fresh air—so he tucked the comforter around her shoulders. Almost instantly she kicked the covering away.

"Why won't you let me protect you?" he whispered. "I won't let you down. Not ever."

Emily twisted and her lips moved soundlessly. Nick put his hand on the swell of her stomach. A faint drum of movement reassured him, and he stroked her soothingly.

"Please, let me take care of you," he said in the same quiet tone. His protective instincts might not be very modern, but that didn't stop him from wanting to guard Emily and their baby in every possible way.

He switched off the small lamp he'd used for reading and slid down next to his wife. Moonlight shone through the lace curtains, turning Emily's hair into a liquid pool of silvery gold. More than ever she looked like an angel. Carefully he gathered her into his arms and pulled the top sheet around them both.

For just a moment he thought Emily stiffened, then she molded herself to him, soft and fragrant. Her breasts were pressed against his chest, and he could feel the slight tautness of her nipples.

An angel?

Right. The sexiest angel that ever lived.

She nudged her knee across his hips and he groaned. It was going to be a long night.

The bright chirp and twitter of birds brought a smile to Nick's mouth as he drifted awake. Nice. Lots better than the morning clatter of breakfast trays and equipment at the hospital.

And he hadn't been holding Emily those other mornings. That was the best part. She lay cuddled next to him beneath the comforter, her head tucked under his chin and their legs tangled together.

Yawning in contentment, Nick looked up and found a pair of yellow feline eyes staring at him. *GeeZee.* Great. Just what he needed.

The cat was curled on the adjacent pillow and he didn't appear any more pleased to see Nick than Nick was happy to see him. The black tip of his tail twitched, and after a session of mutual glaring the feline opened his mouth and spat.

"Beat it, GeeZee," Nick ordered in a quiet but firm tone. "Now."

Obviously GeeZee didn't relate to "quiet but firm." His tail twitched some more, and he hunkered down, his claws flexing in the pillow. His face curled back into a silent feline snarl—it wasn't a pretty sight.

"Nick?" Emily said, stirring sleepily.

"It's okay, Angel." He stroked his hand down her back. "GeeZee and I were trying to decide who's boss."

"Who won?"

"It's still a draw. But I'm bigger than him. And in the pecking order, size matters a lot."

"Oh."

He knew the exact moment Emily became fully awake. One second she was warm and pliant, the next there was tension in every line of her body. Morning sickness?

"How do you feel?" he asked without thinking, then wanted to bite his tongue. Emily didn't appreciate inquiries about her health; she acted like it threatened her independence or something. "Any...er...nausea?" Nick sensed her swallowing.

"None so far."

"Let's stay quiet for a while, just in case," he suggested.

She nodded, and another blissful smile crossed his face. He could spend the next hundred years cupping Emily's bottom. The only problem was GeeZee. He fairly vibrated with suppressed outrage. Strange. Very strange.

Nick cleared his throat. "You said I just got back from a trip. Was I gone long enough for GeeZee to forget me? He's sure acting funny."

"I don't know. Over a month. He's never had trouble before."

A month? Nick was appalled. How could he have left Emily for a month? And when she was pregnant? He thought about the matchbook, with the woman's name and phone number written on it. His stomach roiled and he wondered if morning sickness might be contagious.

"You're mostly a troubleshooter," she continued. "They call you for help when things aren't going right. Otherwise, you'd be gone a lot longer."

"I see. Don't you mind?"

She lifted her head to look at him. "Why should I mind? It's your job, Nick. Something you love doing."

"Yeah, but it leaves you alone an awful lot. I'm more like a temporary fixture in your life than a husband."

Her head dropped like a stone back to his shoulder. "Not...not really," she stuttered. "We spend plenty of time together, and I'd never interfere in your career."

Why not? Nick snapped silently. Which was totally irrational. Most men would have been delighted to have a wife who didn't nag. But not him. No, he wanted Emily to say she needed him at home, not troubleshooting all over the world.

"Meorrrow."

"It's okay, GeeZee," Emily soothed.

The feline licked her hair, though his body remained coiled and he kept a sharp gaze on Nick.

"How come GeeZee? That's an odd name."

"It's short for Godzilla."

All at once GeeZee leaped from the pillow—landing with a thud on Nick's chest—which he then used as a launching pad to the floor. Tail waving in triumph, he sauntered toward the open door. A moment later he thundered down the staircase.

Nick groaned. He was still sore from falling off the roof, and GeeZee weighed a ton. He spit out a strand of fur and rubbed his abused skin.

"See?" she said. "He earned that name. I don't know why anyone would have a cat. They're obnoxious."

He laughed. "Then why do we have GeeZee?"

"GeeZee has m— Us. There's a difference."

Her slight hesitation sent shivers of warning through Nick. She'd started to say, "GeeZee has me." Not that it necessarily meant anything. She could have adopted the cat long before their marriage and would still feel he was *her* cat, as opposed to *their* cat.

Emily shifted slightly, enough to remove her leg from its cozy position across his hips. "I should go to work," she murmured.

"Oh, yeah, the store. Say…why didn't your brother get the business?"

She blinked. "What?"

"You brother, Gabe. He's the oldest son, right?"

"The oldest…?" Emily wiggled out of his grasp and sat up. "That's a completely chauvinistic question, Nicholas Carleton. In the first place, I *bought* the store,

I didn't inherit it. And in the second place, can you imagine Gabe selling kids' clothing or maternity bras?''

"Actually," Nick said calmly. "I can't imagine him at all. Remember...accident, blow to the head, amnesia?''

"I'm not likely to forget," she huffed. "Gabe would die before he'd even set foot in the shop. He's the 'ugh...me man, you woman' type. Though, when it comes to his sister, it's more like 'ugh...me man, you get beer.' I'm surprised he's even standing upright."

"Gosh, I'm overwhelmed by that loving, brother-and-sister bond you share."

A reluctant smile tugged at Emily's mouth. Normally, Nick's not-quite-modern attitudes didn't really bother her. He'd tease her about wanting a wishy-washy nineties kind of guy, and she'd retort it was better than his search for a dumb-as-a-rock fifties sort of gal. Then he'd say, "That all depended on what kind of rock," and the whole thing would disintegrate into an absurd word game.

Unfortunately, these days *normal* was out the window.

It wasn't every day a woman discovers friendship might not be what she wants from her best buddy after all.

No.

Emily shook her head. You didn't mix friendship with sex; it wasn't worth the cost.

She was just confused from finding herself in Nick's arms. He'd been so warm, so very gentle, that she'd imagined other feelings. No wonder. The past few days had been stressful. She'd fully intended to insist on different bedrooms, but they'd still ended up together.

"That's an awfully serious expression, Angel." Nick stroked her cheek, and she glanced at him. His bare chest and muscled shoulders rested comfortably against the pillows. He looked at her intently, and she squirmed.

Okay...maybe it would be worth the risk to their friendship to make love—at least her body thought so. Still, she wasn't going to let out-of-control pregnancy hormones make that kind of decision for her. No, she was going to remain rational and keep from making a big mistake.

"Do you really have to work?" Nick asked. He tugged at the deep vee neck of her gown, his fingers brushing the rising curve of her breast.

Emily drew a sharp breath. "Paige said we should get back to our usual routine." She managed to keep her voice even, but she couldn't do anything about her taut nipples. And because Nick's eyes were focused on her cleavage, he undoubtedly saw the not-so-subtle evidence of her response.

"There's one routine I want to get back to." Nick grinned lazily.

"That isn't what I meant." She felt guilty for trying to escape, but Nick could take care of himself. He seemed completely normal, except for his ardent "husbandly" attentions. The separation might even help him remember, since all he seemed to think about was seducing his "wife" when she was around.

She shook her head. "Gladys will be expecting me."

"Who's Gladys?"

"She's been the head sales clerk for twenty years. I think she knows the business better than I do."

"She must be reliable." Nick put his hands behind his head. "That's good. You can take a few days off and leave everything in her capable hands."

Emily shrugged. "Everyone expects the boss to show

up now and then. And I've been gone a lot since you got hurt. Not that I mind," she said quickly.

"But I'm on vacation," he protested. "We must have planned to spend part of the time together."

Drat. Another pit of quicksand. She hadn't realized how hard it would be to explain the contradictions between what Nick expected and the reality of their separate lives.

"Well, this vacation was kind of unexpected," she said, crossing her fingers in the folds of her long nightgown. "And since I'm going to be gone a lot when the baby comes, we didn't plan to do anything. You know, just working around the house, that sort of thing."

"It's different now," he murmured. "Talk to her. I'll bet she won't mind. Explain that your husband has amnesia and he wants to do a little...remembering."

With a sexy smile Nick swung out of the bed, and Emily's eyes widened. She should have guessed Nick slept in the nude. He didn't seem to have any degree of self-consciousness about her seeing him without his clothes.

Why not? You're married.

Emily moaned and dropped face-first into her pillow. It even smelled like him. Her life was totally screwed up. She'd never be able to face Nick again, not when he got his memory back. She'd keep thinking about how fabulous he looked, bronzed everywhere from the sun except for the narrow strip of skin just below his hips....

A hand caressed her back and she yelped.

"Sorry, Angel, I shouldn't have pushed." Nick sounded genuinely contrite. "I know you don't feel good. Do you need to use the bathroom? I can carry you."

"No. I'm okay." Her voice was muffled from the pillow.

"You're not acting okay."

"I'm all right," she assured. "Really." From the corner of her eye she saw his hard thigh, lightly dusted with hair. She moaned again.

"Angel, I want to help."

Then leave. For an awful moment she thought she'd said the words out loud, but the comforting motion of his hand across her back remained unchanged.

"Maybe I'll take a shower." Emily rolled off the bed. Without a backward glance, she dashed into the bathroom and slammed the door.

Nick prowled through the house restlessly. Despite his most persuasive arguments, Emily had gone to work, but she'd promised to consider a short holiday. In the meantime, he was searching for evidence of his identity.

It was curious, he thought. He liked the house and felt utterly comfortable there. In fact, he couldn't imagine why he'd ever told Emily he *didn't* like it.

Pretty soon he'd be dividing himself between the "old Nick" and the "new Nick." So far, he didn't especially care for the old Nick. It seemed like the only thing he'd done right was marry Emily.

As for his identity...that seemed a little thin. Apparently he didn't accumulate many belongings. His clothes hung in the closet, and there were masculine products in the bathroom. And not much else.

In the backyard he found a ladder lying on the ground, with tools and shingles on the roof above. Nick lifted the ladder with a sense of relief. *Something to do.* He might as well put his "vacation" to good use. His foot was on the first rung when the phone rang.

He muttered a single expletive and strode inside the house. "Yes?" he answered.

"Uh...it's me. How are you doing?"

"Oh. Hi, Angel. I'm keeping busy." Nick winced. He couldn't tell her he planned to finish the roof—she'd pitch a fit.

"I'm sorry about this morning," she said, sounding breathless. "I've talked to Gladys. She'll be happy to cover the store for me. But I need to take care of some things—it'll take most of the afternoon."

"That's fine."

"I left the photo albums out. They might trigger some memories."

Nick nudged the stack of albums, strategically placed on the breakfast table. Emily wanted his amnesia cured almost as much as he did. And, while it seemed perfectly natural she'd want her husband back with his memory intact, it bothered him just the same.

"Okay," Nick agreed, though he doubted it would help. "I'll go through them. See you later."

He sat down and opened a large one marked "Emily's Baby Book." On the first page was a traditional baby-in-the-bathwater shot. He smiled, then laughed when he saw her clad in a clown costume for Halloween. She was adorable.

He fixed himself a cup of coffee and continued through the album. It was intriguing, especially since he couldn't help thinking about his own child. And an unexpected thought occurred to him. *A girl.* He'd like to have a little girl, just like her mother.

The various books progressed through Emily's childhood, and somewhere in the middle a gawky little boy appeared, with hands and feet too big for his body, and eyes that looked hungrily at everyone else, especially

Emily. It didn't take a lot of conjecture to realize the gawky kid was himself.

"Angel," he murmured, touching the plastic-covered pages, "I was right, you became my family."

They looked like nice people. Sometimes exasperated with each other, but full of fun and the pleasures of living. People he wanted to remember. They seemed familiar, similar to images from a subconscious dream.

The last two albums were messier, with odd mementos stuck inside—pieces of ribbon, a dried flower, even a flattened-out bottle cap. Most of the photos were of Emily, or both of them. It reassured him to a certain extent, because he couldn't doubt the honest affection reflected in the photographs.

A frown tightened his forehead as he turned a page and saw a collection of wedding pictures. Emily was luminous in white lace and silk, but the groom had been carefully clipped out of every photo.

"What the hell is going on?"

Nick slapped the book onto the table. Apparently there were a few things he needed to discuss with his wife. He grabbed the phone and dialed the number Emily had left. He snarled at the irritating bleep of a busy signal.

Five minutes later it was still busy.

"Damnation."

Fuming wouldn't help. But he spent several minutes cursing, anyway. The doorbell clanged and he stomped to the front door, muttering beneath his breath. Terrific. Hank McAllister, the leering policeman, waited on the porch.

"Hey, buddy," Hank said. "It's my day off. Thought I'd come by and see how you're doing."

Nick gritted his teeth. "Except for a few holes in my

memory, I'm fine. Sorry, I can't chat. I have to work on the roof."

His "old friend" gave him an amiable grin. "Yeah...that's what I figured you'd be doing when I saw Emily's Blazer downtown. I'll help."

He started to say no, but Hank was persistent. Nick soon found himself working on the roof over the porch, enjoying the hot sunshine and listening to Hank's easy conversation.

Hell, what do you know? He liked the guy. And besides, his old pal might be able to shed some light on a few of the mysteries he'd uncovered.

"I appreciate the help," he said.

Hank tossed a damaged shingle to the ground. "No problem. Besides, this way we might get it done before Emily comes home." He paused and grinned again. "You may have noticed she has a temper. If she catches you up here, you might as well jump headfirst, because she's going to kill you, anyway."

Nick laughed. He was still angry and worried, yet Hank's simple good humor was infectious. And it was undoubtedly true...if Emily found him on the roof she'd trip a circuit breaker.

Stubborn little thing, his Angel.

Nick fitted a new shingle into place and fastened it home with a few hard, fast blows. He shouldn't do anything to upset her, but the image of those wedding photos flitted through his mind, and his fingers clenched around the hammer.

With any luck they'd finish the roof before she arrived—which meant he'd have time to cool down. Calm and rational was much better than furious and paranoid.

Maybe they'd had a fight and she'd cut them up in the heat of the moment. Or there might be some other reasonable explanation. It didn't seem logical that she'd push him to look at the albums, knowing what he'd find.

"Let's see," he said slowly. "We've known each other since high school? You and me and Emily's brother?"

Hank gave him a curious glance. "Fifth grade, actually. God, this is weird. You really don't remember, do you?"

"No."

"Phew." Hank handed him another shingle. "You don't seem any different. And you're not freaked out or anything. That's pretty good."

Nick shrugged. "Actually, I'm mostly worried about what this is doing to Emily. It can't be good for her or the baby."

Hank nodded sympathetically.

They worked in silence for a while, then Nick cleared his throat. "You know Emily pretty well, right?"

Hank looked up. "Sure. She was a pesky tagalong when we were kids, then overnight she turned into this luscious little..." His voice trailed at Nick's scowl. "That is, she became a very attractive woman."

Nick tried to remember that Hank was his friend and wouldn't appreciate getting punched in the mouth. "Seems like we waited a long time before getting together."

"Yeah, that seemed funny. You were always buddies. But then, she was pretty skittish after her divorce. I didn't think she'd ever get married again."

Divorce? Nick felt like he'd been poleaxed. "When did Emily get divorced?" he asked, trying to sound nonchalant. After all, it was the only explanation. And a lot better than some of the unlikely alternatives he'd imagined. So why did it annoy the hell out of him?

Dismay filled the other man's face. "Damn. This amynesia stuff is tricky. I suppose you haven't discussed her divorce yet?"

Nick shook his head. "What about it?"

"Well, right after college Emily worked for an advertising agency in the city. She married some guy at the firm. It was a real disaster—only lasted a year. That's all I know."

"I thought—"

An exasperated shriek rose from the ground below. "Nicholas Carleton, what are you doing?"

Hank groaned and looked like he wanted to crawl under one of the shingles they'd just replaced.

"I see you up there, Hank McAllister."

"I'm dead meat," Hank mumbled. "You'd better jump, there isn't any way out of this now."

"I'm not going without a fight," Nick said stoically.

Hank slumped back on the roof and put his hand across his heart. "I'm done for. I should have listened to my instructors. First day at the academy they said, 'Don't get in the middle of a domestic dispute—it's too dangerous.' They were right. If I live I'll have to tell them."

"I said we were getting a roofer, and I meant it. How dare you go up there after what happened?" Emily's tone bordered on hysterical.

"I'm fine. And I'm not a child, I just have amnesia," Nick snapped, getting angry again himself.

"You have amnesia because you fell off the roof. And now you're back up there. You might get dizzy. Anything could happen."

Emily planted her hands on her hips, fairly steaming with outrage. A corner of Nick's mind appreciated the sight she made, her cheeks bright with ire and haloed by that glorious gold hair. She wore a sophisticated, teal silk dress that wrapped in the front, leaving a deep vee at the neck. He remembered when she'd put it on that morning, talking about how it accentuated the positive and concealed the negative. The negative being her stomach.

He didn't understand women.

How could her pregnancy be a "negative" when she was so happy about the baby?

Nick rubbed his temple. Questions, always questions. He looked at Emily again, and a part of his brain flipped, like he was seeing something in double focus. He'd seen her from the roof before...but that time she'd been smiling at him.

It wasn't much, just a shred of memory. And certainly no help in dealing with the current situation.

"Well?" Emily demanded.

"I'm the husband," he said. "Husbands fix roofs, they clean out rain gutters, and they screw up the plumbing. Get used to it."

"Get used to it? Used to it! You...you..." Words apparently failing her, she spun on her heel and marched into the house.

Hank whistled. "Great work. We're still alive. Have you ever considered a career in law enforcement, or maybe family counseling? That bit about fixing the plumbing was certainly a selling point. I'll have to remember it if I ever get married myself."

Ignoring him, Nick climbed down the ladder and followed Emily. They needed to talk, and if they had to do some yelling in the meantime, then fine. They would yell a little.

"Emily?"

A wet dishrag hit him in the face.

Okay. They would yell a lot.

Chapter Six

"Thanks a lot." Nick tossed the wet towel into the sink and faced his wife.

Emily glared at him and went back to scrubbing the stove. Since the appliance was spotless, he couldn't see much point to the project. "How could you go back up on that roof?" she muttered angrily. "You know how I feel about it. But no, you had to pull a stupid macho stunt."

"Gee," he drawled. "Aren't you supposed to be walking on verbal eggshells? God knows what you could do to my damaged psyche. I thought you were supposed to be nice to me. Diplomatic and careful about everything you say."

"Nice? What a joke. But everything's a joke to you, Nick. Right? That's just the problem. Getting on the roof, making love—even amnesia is a joke."

Nick tried to hang on to his temper. "We agreed not to raise old arguments."

"This isn't an *old* argument, this is a *new* argument."

She looked at him, eyes stormy. "You could have been killed that day. Or broken your neck, or done some other permanent damage. Then you go right back up there."

"Nothing happened."

"But something could have. And now you act like it's some sort of game."

He took a deep breath. "I know it isn't a game. But you seem to think we should put our life on hold until I get my memory back. I don't have any intention of doing that."

"Paige said it would be only a few days and then you'll be back to normal."

"Bully for her." Nick paused. "From what the doctors say, *nobody* knows that much about amnesia. I might remember, I might not. In the meantime, I'm getting that roof fixed."

Emily stared at Nick, alarm swamping all other emotions. This was the second time he'd talked about not getting his memory back. If he didn't remember, things could be different between them.

They could even have a real marriage....

No.

She swallowed and stumbled to the sink. No matter what happened, she couldn't appropriate Nick's life. They might be married, but it wasn't real. Sooner or later he'd have to know the truth. And the truth was, Nick didn't love her. Not that way.

"Paige said there were other treatments," she said, her voice muffled by the rush of tap water. "If your memory didn't return naturally."

"What kind of treatments?"

"Hypnosis maybe. And there's some drug therapies they might try. She didn't tell you because she didn't think it would be necessary."

"Would it be so terrible if I didn't remember?" Nick asked quietly. "Hank says I seem just the same as ever. I care about you, and I care about the baby. Nothing has to change."

Emily turned off the faucet and dried her hands. She waited a long moment before turning around. "Everything changes. But it isn't as though we have to make any decisions. This situation is temporary. It won't last." She faced Nick and made a helpless gesture.

"Somehow, I don't find that reassuring."

Emily rubbed the back of her neck. "When you remember, you'll understand."

His face darkened. "I understand you're pushing me away, but you won't explain why. What is it, Emily? Are we really married?" he asked bluntly.

Her head jerked back. "Of course we're married. I'll get the certificate, if that's what you want."

"Of course?" Nick repeated through gritted teeth. He grabbed a paper towel and wiped the sweat from his face and neck. He didn't want to say anything he'd regret. It was a hot day and they both needed to cool off, in more ways than one. He pointed at her. "Explain something then, Angel. Why do you fidget with your wedding ring so much? And why does it look so new?"

Emily pulled her hands apart, guilt flooding her blue eyes. "I...I forget to wear it. I take it off to cook or clean, and then it just sits on the counter. I don't like rings."

"That isn't just *any* ring," he ground out.

"Oh, right. You seem to think it's a brand or something," she snapped back.

"No. It just seems strange you'd still be uncomfortable after wearing the thing for five months." Nick gave Emily a challenging stare. He wanted...*needed*, to know what was really going on between them. "Tell me you love me."

"I...love you."

"It would be a lot more effective if you looked me in the eye and said, 'I'm deeply in love with you, Nick. We're a great team.'"

She looked at him. "I love you. We're a great team."

Damn. He believed her, and yet...he didn't. "Get the certificate," he said, defeated. He needed proof. He wanted something tangible, showing Emily was really his wife.

Though Emily scowled rebelliously, she stalked from the kitchen and returned with a large envelope. She handed it to him without a word and immediately started scrubbing the front of the refrigerator. Like the stove, it didn't seem to be in need of attention, but he supposed she wanted an outlet for her frustration.

Almost reluctantly, he opened the envelope and pulled out a creamy-colored certificate.

"Groom...Nicholas Carleton."

"Bride...Emily Carmichael."

A copy of the wedding license was attached. The date seemed right. There were witnesses and everything. It appeared very legal and appropriate. Also cold and impersonal. No pictures, no pressed flowers, none of the sentimental trivia he might have thought Emily would keep.

"We were married by a judge?" he queried, glancing at the officiating signature.

Emily blew a strand of hair away from her forehead. "Yes. We didn't want a big to-do, just a simple ceremony. It was a decision we *both* made," she said pointedly.

Nick thought about the wedding pictures in the album.

Emily in white lace, radiant with expectation. Flowers. A five-tiered cake. The traditional garter belt on her silky thigh. Another man putting his ring on her finger.

Ice condensed in his stomach.

"You mean," he said carefully, "nothing fancy or special or traditional like your first wedding?"

Her mouth dropped, and she cast a heated glance at the ceiling. "Hank," she muttered.

"No, those damned photo albums."

"What do you mean? I threw everything away from my first wedding," Emily sputtered. "I wouldn't own a picture of Kevin to save my life. He was a snake."

Kevin. Well at least he'd gotten the man's name.

"Angel, I don't know about your Kevin, but the wedding photos are right there." Nick pointed at the table and the album lying on top of the stack.

"He's not *my* Kevin," she muttered. But she picked up the book and opened it. Her eyes grew even wider as she flicked through the pages. "The groom is cut out."

"Oh, news flash."

She ignored him. "I don't understand. This belongs to you. Er...it's an album you kept before we got married. Why would you want to keep these old wedding photos?"

"Got me," Nick said carelessly. "So, why didn't you tell me about the snake? I'd think an ex-husband is a valid conversation topic."

Emily rolled her eyes. "You've had amnesia for less than a week. There are lots of things we haven't discussed."

"Start discussing. I'm all ears."

"What? You want confessions?" Emily was tempted

to hit Nick over the head herself. Anything would be better than this inquisition.

"I want to know about Kevin."

She clenched her jaw. "Kevin is past tense. He's been out of my life for over ten years."

"Why did you get divorced? Do you still love him?"

"What? You're crazy."

Instead of hitting him or saying something she'd regret, she opted for retreat. Furious, strategic retreat. She stomped out of the house and slammed the door so hard the windows rattled. Outside it was bright and sunny, but she barely noticed as she marched down the street.

Nick had a lot of nerve questioning her past. Even if their marriage was normal he wouldn't have the right to be so suspicious. Lots of people had ex-spouses. Besides, the *real* Nick knew all about Kevin.

It wasn't any secret, just an ugly part of her life that was done and over with. Actually, she didn't even hate Kevin anymore. She was just embarrassed about being so naive. She'd married a jerk. Big deal. It happened all the time.

But right now she wasn't sure which of the men she'd married was the biggest jerk.

Not fair.

So what? she argued with her conscience. Nick would understand when he got his memory back.

If he gets it back.

"Shut up," she said aloud, earning an alarmed stare from a neighbor, who was sitting on her porch. "Hi, Mrs. Pickering," she called, waving automatically.

Mrs. Pickering pulled at Mr. Pickering's arm and whispered in his ear. She was a sweet old woman with a tongue faster than the information superhighway.

Within an hour, all of western Washington would know that Emily Carleton had started talking to herself.

"Emily!" Nick shouted.

Emily kept walking. She didn't want to talk to her husband. She didn't even want to think about him, but that appeared to be impossible.

"Husband," she muttered in dismay. Four days ago she wouldn't have automatically thought of Nick as her husband. Buddy. Pal. Friend. Annoying wretch she was fond of...but not her husband. A piece of paper didn't make a marriage, and a fantasy world, invented because of his amnesia, couldn't make them into the perfect couple. Paige didn't know how much she'd been asking with that "You've got to pretend you're married for real" business.

If only Emily could explain, but Nick was right about one thing—there weren't any experts on amnesia. Telling him might cause permanent damage to his memory. She couldn't take that risk.

"Dammit, Emily!" Nick lunged around her and caught her shoulders. She distantly recognized that despite his anger, he was careful not to shake or startle her too much. She should have felt protected, yet it only meant he was thinking about the baby.

"We have to talk," he said. "You can't just walk out."

"We don't have anything to talk about."

"That isn't true. Angel, I know this is hard. I can't remember things, and you're unsettled because of the pregnancy, but that—"

"I told you, I don't like being patronized. So I'm pregnant. I'm supposed to be emotional, but it doesn't incapacitate me or make me unreasonable. Or not that much," she added, wanting to be honest.

But since she didn't have any particular place to go—and didn't want to fight with her husband in front of the main gossip pipeline of Crockett—she turned around and headed back up the block.

"Emily, dear," Mrs. Pickering called, scurrying out to the sidewalk. "Hello, Nick. This is so nice. I hardly ever get to see you. You do seem to travel a lot. Though...I suppose with the baby coming you'll be home more often."

Nick smiled politely.

Emily put her hand on her abdomen and wondered what terrible thing she'd done to deserve the past four days. It must have been a doozy. A real barn burner. The baby kicked in apparent agreement.

"Are you all right?" Nick asked in a low undertone.

"Oh, sure." *I love having my life messed up.*

"Mr. P. said there was an ambulance at your place on Saturday. What happened?" Mrs. Pickering asked, her alert gaze shifting between them. "Nothing serious, I hope?"

"No." Emily forced a polite smile of her own. "Nick fell off the roof and spent a couple days in the hospital. But as you can see, he's fine now."

The other woman shook her head and patted Emily's arm. "These men of ours. They keep us on our toes, but I guess they're worth keeping. Aren't they, dear?"

"Oh...yes. Nick is certainly in a class by himself," Emily murmured.

A shade of wry amusement twisted Nick's mouth. He put his arm around her shoulders. "It's warm out, Angel. I think you need to get inside."

"That's right! Come in for a glass of iced tea," Mrs. Pickering declared immediately. "You know," she said in a confidential tone to Nick. "With Emily's parents retired to California and her brothers and sisters scattered about, Mr. P. and I think of ourselves as family. You can always count on us, any time of the day or night.''

''That's...kind of you,'' Nick said.

''As for these little spats—'' Mrs. Pickering tittered and seemed mildly abashed. ''I'm sorry, but I couldn't help noticing you were have a disagreement. You'll find that everything works out, though. Why, Mr. P. and I used to argue all the time, and just look at us now.'' She waved at the porch. ''Utter tranquillity.''

Obediently they looked at Mr. Pickering, snoozing beneath the cooling breeze of an oscillating fan. Emily happened to know that ''Mr. P.'' had achieved tranquillity by a case of selective deafness—he could hear everything except his wife.

''Just listen to me, young man,'' Mrs. Pickering said, offering her advice in the sagest of manners. ''Emily may be touchy for the next few months, but when you see that baby it won't matter a bit. Now you come into the house, and I'll tell you all about these women things. Oh my, I remember the times I was expecting.''

Nick gave Emily a helpless, pleading glance.

Emily was tempted to let him dangle in the elderly woman's clutches, but figured she'd be dangling right along with him. ''Thanks for the invitation, Mrs. Pickering, but it's time for my nap.'' She stroked her stomach. ''Doctor's orders.''

Nick's eyes gleamed at the word *nap*, and she wanted to kick him. Men! Couldn't they think about anything but sex? Here they were, in the middle of a fight, and he'd gotten that unmistakable bedroom look on his face.

She maintained her artificial smile until they were back in the house, then she crossed her arms and glared. Nick didn't even have the good grace to appear chagrined. He just leaned against the closed door and raised his eyebrows.

"Time for your nap, Angel."

"I'm not taking a nap, and you darn well know it!"

He clucked. "Darn? That's pretty strong. I thought you didn't like such language in front of our baby."

"We're having a fight," Emily reminded him furiously. "I'm glad you think it's so funny."

Nick took several deep breaths and pushed away from the door. It was his fault she was upset. He hadn't been thrilled to learn of Emily's first marriage, so he'd overreacted. "I'm just trying to get some perspective." He put one hand on her hip and cupped the back of her neck with the other.

Emily's eyes flashed furiously, but he pulled her to him, anyway.

"Show me what you feel," he whispered against her lips. "I can't know without your help."

"You don't need to know anything. Leave me alone."

"I can't. You're my wife." He kissed her gently. "It was a lousy reason to fight. I'm sorry."

"Nick," she protested, yet her hands crept about his waist. "We can't."

He kissed her neck. "It's all right, Angel. I talked to Dr. Wescott...we won't hurt the baby. We'll go real slow, and we'll stop if it's uncomfortable. I promise, I'd never hurt you."

"That isn't...I'm not..." Emily's words trailed as he enveloped her with his strength and warmth.

He widened his stance, cradling her between his legs. Shimmering heat swept through her as his hard arousal pressed against her abdomen. Unable to stop herself, Emily rubbed against him. He groaned and they rocked together in sultry counterpoint, sharing both the pleasure and sweet agony of being close, yet not close enough.

This isn't me, she thought. *I'm not wild or uninhibited.*

Nick trailed an open, biting kiss down her neck and she trembled.

Well...maybe a little wild, Emily decided. She tried to get closer, but the swell of her stomach intruded. "I'm so big," she muttered.

Nick stroked her tummy, his work-hardened hand catching the silk of her dress. The soft cloth slid upward until she could feel the roughness of his jeans against her bare thighs. "You're wonderful and sexy and perfect."

"How can you say that? I get bigger every day. It's like instant pregnancy the past couple of weeks. Sexy?" Emily shook her head. "You're just confused."

"I'm not confused. Maybe I'm seeing things more clearly than ever before. Angel..." He lifted her chin and gazed into her worried eyes. "If I did something that messed up our marriage, I want a second chance."

"You didn't do anything. When you remember—"

Nick slid his thumb across Emily's mouth, stopping the words. "Don't say that. Don't think about amnesia. Don't think about anything but us—right here, right now."

"Please, Nick," Emily said his name again, breathing it over and over between kisses. It was her responsibility to keep things sane and rational until his memory returned. No matter how much she wanted to blame Nick, it wasn't really his fault, not even the misunderstanding about her first marriage.

He cupped her bottom, pulling her into even more intimate alignment with his body. She shuddered. Of their own accord, her hands tugged at his shirt, pulling the tail out from the top of his jeans. He was strong and hard. An exciting stranger...yet still Nick. Tentatively her fingers splayed across the sleek heat of his back. She wanted to touch him, but it seemed dangerous, too.

"Yes," he whispered, and then his hands were everywhere, touching and teasing. The dizzy rush of her blood faltered at his urgency. It wasn't going to be any different with Nick. No matter what he said, he would go too fast and leave her behind. And she'd be left frustrated and empty, feeling like a failure because she couldn't fully respond.

You can't stop now. He'd never understand.

Her thoughts scattered as Nick eased them both down on the wide couch. He arranged her over his body and kissed her again...one of those long, drugging kisses that made everything mushy in her head.

But you'll be sorry if you don't, a contradictory, inner voice warned.

Oh, be quiet, Emily thought crossly, weary of complicated decisions. But she knew the voice was right. He *wouldn't* understand if she stopped him, and they'd *both* be sorry later if she didn't.

Her dress hiked up as she straddled his hips, trying one last time to bring some sense into the situation. "Nick," she said shakily.

He smiled...a slow, sexy, confident smile. "Yes?"

"We shouldn't. I mean, Hank—"

"Went home."

Emily's tongue flicked across her dry lips, and Nick's gaze followed the small movement. He lifted his legs, shifting her forward. For a long, intense moment she stared into the face of the man she knew so well. She could hardly remember a time when he hadn't been in her life. Her heart slowly turned over and her eyes filled with tears.

"Angel...don't," Nick said softly. "Please don't cry. What's wrong?"

"I'm scared," she admitted, drawing a shaky breath. "Just a little."

"Of me?" His hands stroked over her in sensual persuasion. "Of hurting the baby?"

Of losing you. She shook her head, fearful of speaking the words aloud. Too much—and too little—had already been said. She'd never really understood how important Nick was to her...so completely a part of her life and heart.

"What?"

"I...I'm not..." Emily caught her bottom lip between her teeth. Worry began creeping into Nick's face—she had to say something. But he was too smart to accept a lame excuse.

"Angel?"

"Uh...I'm not very good at this. I mean, we haven't been married long enough to...er...work out the bugs." She avoided looking at him. "In bed...that is. I'm slightly inhibited. It's not your fault." She shrugged miserably. The confession contained a mixture of truth and fiction. It was the truth part she disliked admitting the most.

"And I haven't been here enough." He touched her cheek apologetically. "I should have stayed home if we were having problems."

"I said it wasn't your fault." Irritation colored her voice. Drat the man. How could he annoy and melt her at the same time?

"Of course it is. No wonder you gave me those excuses about not making love. But I'll make it all right, Angel."

"*Men*," she muttered, though his conclusion neatly let her off the hook for her procrastination. The breath caught in her throat as the heat of Nick's mouth covered her breast. Moisture seeped through the thin fabric of her silk dress. Distantly she recognized his handiwork in removing her bra, because it was certainly missing.

"My bra."

"You don't need it."

"You're impossible."

He tugged at the front of her dress until it gaped open, then he smiled at the display. Emily's breasts tightened and desire pulsed between her legs.

"Well, heck. It worked," he murmured. "You're not scared anymore."

His male arrogance galled her, almost as much as the confession of her sexual inhibitions had done. But she didn't have time to think about it. The tip of Nick's tongue swirled around one nipple and she moaned. When his head dropped back onto the sofa cushions—breaking the contact—she shimmied upward against his chest. If their friendship was going down the drain, she might as well enjoy the moment...as far as it went.

"I'll have to start wearing teddies," she said. "Something you can't get off so easily."

"Don't count on it. I think I like challenges."

He trailed his finger down her neck, circling each of her breasts without touching their sensitive peaks. Emily bit her lip against another moan. Did he know what he was doing to her?

Deep in her heart she still wasn't sure if making love with Nick would be any different—but it was too late to stop. Maybe it had always been too late.

If only she wasn't pregnant...it might be better. But if she wasn't pregnant, they wouldn't be married. And if they weren't married, Nick wouldn't think they had a normal relationship, and they wouldn't be about to make love. He'd be a good friend with amnesia, nothing more.

Complicated.

Like their friendship.

"Trust me, Angel," Nick whispered. "If it doesn't feel right, we'll try something new."

Emily rested her forehead on his chest. *Something new?* She couldn't admit that *everything* was new, because this was their first time together.

He tugged at the hidden fastening of her dress, and it slithered from her shoulders. She obliged by shrugging her arms from the sleeves. The silken fabric pooled about her hips. With a small smile Nick touched the lacy elastic of her French-cut underwear, pulled tautly over her stomach.

"Nice," he murmured. "Very sexy."

"It...it's special maternity wear, but my customers say it's not too comfortable after the fifth or sixth month," she said, shivering as he slid his finger beneath the thin band.

The sensual intensity in Nick's eyes gentled. "You shouldn't wear anything that doesn't feel right. It'll be hard enough carrying the baby."

A wry smile touched her lips. "You mean I'll be so huge, why bother with sexy stuff, anyway?"

With a sigh, Nick reluctantly abandoned the tempting scrap of lace over Emily's hip and grasped her shoulders. "We're in this together," he said quietly. "The size of the father has a lot to do with the size of the baby. I'm a large man, you're a small woman. Of course you'll get big, it's only natural. You'll also be gorgeous, even if you wear a potato sack.''

"And that's exactly what I'll be wearing in a few months,'' she muttered. "A potato sack.''

"Angel!''

He was relieved to hear her laugh—a sweet, slightly embarrassed sound.

"Okay,'' she said. "It's just that I've wanted children for years, and now I look at myself in the mirror and wonder if I was crazy.''

"Not crazy,'' he murmured. "Perfect.''

The warm approval in Nick's expression bolstered Emily's confidence...and reminded her she was nearly naked—something she was certain *he* hadn't overlooked.

"Just wait until you see those nursing bras I'll have to wear,'' she retorted, forgetting that Nick wasn't about to see any nursing bras. After today she'd probably lose him completely. "You'll wonder what you ever saw in me.''

"Not a chance.''

"Of course, I didn't wear these panties for you,'' she said virtuously, wanting to strike a blow for independent womanhood.

"I know,'' he agreed.

She looked at him suspiciously. "Men think women wear this stuff for them, but it isn't that at all. We wear it for ourselves.''

"I see.'' All at once he sat up, deftly lifting her from his lap.

She grabbed his shoulders. "Nick?''

"It's okay. I'm just taking this production upstairs. It'll be better in bed. You'll be more comfortable.''

"I can walk.''

He laughed softly, tugging at the loose dress until it

fell with a swish to the ground. "I know you can walk, but I don't want to let go."

Never had Emily been more aware of the implicit power and strength in Nick's body than when he carried her up the staircase. Her weight didn't seem to hinder him, and he laid her on the bed, breathing easily until his gaze swept her form.

"Angel," he whispered. "You're incredible."

Emily closed her eyes.

"I've been working and I'm sweaty—I really should take a shower first," he continued, stroking the curves and angles of her body with something close to awe. "But I'm afraid to let you out of my sight."

"Then don't," she whispered. She reached out blindly and felt him come down on the mattress beside her. "Don't leave me."

Don't give me a chance to back out. I don't want to do any more thinking or deciding or questioning.

The hunger for him had been building since that first kiss in the hospital. Maybe it was because of the baby—a false intimacy because it was Nick's child she carried in her womb—but she wanted him. Right or wrong. Friendship be damned.

Nick helped Emily as she unbuttoned his shirt, and groaned as she unzipped his jeans, dragging them down his legs with his briefs. He wanted to take things slowly, but she wasn't making it easy.

"Angel, it's all right. Easy," he soothed. He caught her fingers before they could close around him.

"Don't you want—"

"I want it to last. And if you touch me, it won't last two seconds." He curled over and around her, letting her feel the rigid strength of his passion. "I'm not going anywhere."

"Oh, Nick…" Her words ended in a keening sigh as he caught her nipple between his lips. He suckled lightly, then drew a damp line with his tongue to her other breast, giving it the same gentle treatment. Emily wiggled beneath him.

"What do you want?" he asked hoarsely. "You have to tell me."

"I…" Faint color touched her face.

"Yes?"

Emily shook her head, closing her eyes again. Nick raised himself up to look at her, and desire clawed at his self-control. Her gold hair was tumbled wildly across the scattered pillows, and her beautiful, ripe body was arched in the filtered light through the windows.

"Tell me what feels best to you."

He swept his hand down her length. Except for her panties she was completely naked. Hooking his fingers into the lacy elastic, he eased them down her legs. The scent of feminine arousal filled his senses.

"Angel?" Nick came down next to Emily again, but she still refused to look at him. "Do you like this?" He nuzzled her breasts again, still lightly, still teasing them with light strokes of his tongue and fingers.

Emily trembled beneath him, stirring restlessly. Still silent.

He kissed her taut belly and sensed the faint movement of their baby beneath his cheek. "She's kicking."

"She?"

"Hmm. I don't know why, but I'm sure it's a girl. A perfect little girl, just like her mother."

"Oh."

Nick eased upward and kissed Emily, dipping his tongue into her mouth like a man dying of thirst. For an endless moment he reveled in the taste of her, the luxury of knowing that however long it took, he'd join their bodies in the deepest way possible...but not before he learned what pleased her. When the kiss ended they were both breathing hard.

"Tell me," he insisted again. "Tell me what you like."

He looked at her and noted the restless shifting of her legs, the tight rise of her breasts. He remembered the quiet, desperate sounds she'd made when he suckled her. A wild heat filled his eyes.

"This?" he said, circling the tip of her breasts with his thumbs, barely brushing the velvet peaks.

She squirmed.

"More?"

"Nick!"

"Mmm." Nick tasted her. Still lightly. Still without substance to the caress.

Color suffused Emily's skin, radiating from the twin mounds he held so carefully. "I hate you," she muttered.

Relenting, he put his mouth over her right breast, drawing hard on the tip—enough to give pleasure, yet not to cause pain. Emily moaned and nearly came off the bed. A dark, primitive delight swept over him. She tasted so good, felt so good, he could hold her like this forever.

After giving equal attention to both breasts, Nick looked at Emily and smiled. "You enjoy that, don't you?"

She nodded once, jerkily, as though shocked by her own response.

"Why is it so hard to tell me?"

"I...we've known each other for so long. It wasn't...it hasn't always been like this."

Nick nodded, as well, thinking he understood. "Well, Angel, we're changing things." He bent over her again. "And you're going to like it."

He loved her then, loved her into a twisting flame of need and passion. When he finally slipped between her legs he thought he'd explode.

"Is it all right?" he asked urgently. "The book said it was okay, but my weight...is it too much?"

Emily shook her head frantically. "No.... Please, Nick. Now. Don't wait."

But he made her wait, just a moment longer to be certain it was right, then took her in a single, powerful thrust.

The pleasure was so sharp that the difference between pain and paradise was almost indistinguishable. And then he moved inside of her, sheathed in ecstasy, feeling the rippling contractions of Emily's fulfillment sweep them both into pure, liquid fire.

And somehow he knew it had never been like this before—not with any other woman.

Chapter Seven

A rumbling sound and vibration drilled into Nick's consciousness. He opened his eyes and blinked. A moment later memories of the previous night poured through him. He smiled and lifted his head.

"Emily?"

No Emily.

The space next to him on the bed was empty. Nick dropped his head back to the pillow, still smiling. A tiny movement drew his attention, and he looked down at GeeZee, tucked in his armpit. The feline purred smugly.

"What? No threats? No claw action?"

GeeZee licked his paw and half closed his eyes—the epitome of a contented, fat cat.

"I'm surprised, pal. You have a lot more to be jealous about today than yesterday."

GeeZee yawned, rolled the balance of his considerable weight against Nick's chest and fell asleep. As a conversationalist, he lacked something.

"Sheesh." Nick rolled his eyes. Cats were like

women—you couldn't figure them out, no matter how hard you tried. He'd have sworn GeeZee would be resentful, especially after getting kicked off the bed in the middle of night...and again at five that morning.

But *no.*

GeeZee acted like everything was hunky-dory again. Which it was, of course.

Nick's smile turned euphoric. He'd lost track of the number of times he and Emily had made love. The bed, the couch after a midnight snack, the shower....

Yeah, the shower had been great. Emily, all wet and slick on top of him, the water turning her hair to burnished bronze. A man could get spoiled by that much heaven.

Too bad it was only going to last forever.

As for his memory...Nick shrugged. If it came back, it came back. If it didn't, then they'd deal with it, though he figured he'd handle it better than Emily. She got awfully upset when he suggested the possibility of never remembering.

Rolling free of the snoring feline monster, he got up, filled with a sense of well-being. His marriage—and his life—seemed to be going exactly the way any man could hope. He donned a pair of briefs and sauntered out in search of his wife.

"Angel?"

"Down here," she called, sounding breathless.

He saw her sitting at the foot of the staircase, dressed in shorts and a T-shirt, using the wall for support in some kind of exercise, her hair tumbling in a silken cloud over her shoulders. A towel was looped about her bare left foot with a pillow supporting the same thigh. She held the ends of the towel with one hand and stretched, arching her body in a very provocative manner.

Delicious.

Incredibly delicious.

Pregnant or not, Emily moved with instinctive grace. He sat on the fourth step from the bottom, savoring the view. "Should you be doing that?" he asked finally.

Emily blew a strand of hair from her forehead. "Sure. Why not?"

"I don't know. What if you hurt yourself?"

She wrinkled her nose at him. "Not likely. My obstetrician prescribed these exercises. He thinks labor might be easier, and I'll recover faster after the birth if I get specific muscles in shape."

"Oh."

Nick watched for another few minutes...and found his briefs becoming tight. After making love for hours on end he should have been a little less eager, but his wife was in a class by herself. The satin warmth of her skin and her supple, eager responses were burned into his soul. He wasn't sure he'd ever be complete again without his Angel.

"Are you going to take a bath when you're finished?" he asked huskily, envisioning another feast of underwater fun. Emily reveled in water. She really loved the stuff. They even had an enormous, whirlpool bathtub in the remodeled bathroom that gave new meaning to the word *clean.*

"I'm not getting that sweaty," she retorted.

"I know."

"You..." Emily looked at Nick, then quickly ducked her head. Despite her misgivings, making love with Nick had shattered and rebuilt every concept she'd had of herself. And of Nick. He was tender, playful, erotic and incredibly stupendous. If it hadn't been for impending doom, the night would have been perfect.

She wanted to surrender and enjoy the moment, but reality was too close. Any minute she expected his eyes to widen with shock and recognition.

It made her nervous.

So did seeing him in next to nothing. Nick didn't look like a husband, he looked like a world-class hunk. Sex incarnate. No way was he going to trade his globe-hopping, woman-in-every-port life for a pregnant wife in plain old Crockett, Washington.

Brother. Why did she have to depress herself?

"Any morning sickness?" Nick asked, leaning back on one elbow.

"Nope. I got lucky today." Emily finished her stretching routine and rested against the wall. Noticing Nick's appreciative examination of her legs, she tugged at her shorts and smoothed her T-shirt over her rounded tummy. "I...uh, I'm glad you were able to sleep late."

"It would have been nice waking up together," he murmured.

"Then we would have spent the day in bed," she retorted.

"See? A perfect plan. Let's go back and pretend." He nudged her knee with his foot and wiggled his eyebrows.

Emily tossed the towel at him, both embarrassed and flattered by his rapt attention and conspicuous arousal.

"I guess the answer is no," he said.

She laughed and shook her head. "The answer is definitely no. And don't tell me you're going back on the roof as an alternative. My heart can't take the pressure."

"I never wanted to scare you." Nick leaned forward, lightly clasping his hands between his knees and gazing at her intently. "You know that, don't you?"

Emily couldn't doubt Nick. Even with amnesia, she didn't believe he'd lie to her. "I know."

At her assurance he nodded, but his forehead remained creased in thought. "Please don't get upset, but I can't help wondering about your first husband."

Emily shifted uncomfortably. "Why do you want to know about Kevin?"

"I'm not trying to start another fight, but I don't want to make the same mistake he did. I want to understand." Nick's brown eyes were concerned, not accusing, and she relaxed.

"Believe me, you couldn't possibly make his mistakes. You're far too decent."

That made him smile. "Thanks."

She smiled, too, then shrugged her shoulders. "I've always felt foolish for not seeing what Kevin was really like. It didn't take me long after we were married."

"Hank said it ended after a year?"

"I would have sworn it lasted a lifetime," she murmured dryly. "Seemed like it, anyway. I knew it was a mistake within a month."

"Why did you stay?"

Emily shivered, as unwelcome memories threatened the peace she'd found. Nick instantly slid down the steps. He pulled her across his legs and cuddled her close. His big hand rubbed her stomach—a wordless promise to keep every trace of harm or distress away from her and the baby.

"Don't worry, Angel. You don't have to tell me."

Emily put her head on his shoulder and felt the solid, comforting thump of his heart beneath her cheek. She knew the "real" Nick honestly cared about her. He was protective in an aggravating, big-brother kind of way.

But not like this.

Not like her pain and happiness were the same as his own.

She kissed his jaw, her lips lingering against the rasp of his morning beard. Sexy. Elemental. Unable to resist, she flicked her tongue against his skin.

"Angel," he groaned. Almost imperceptibly, his embrace changed. Less comforting. More sultry. Bringing an awareness of bare legs against bare legs and the pleasing differences between feminine and masculine textures.

Emily trembled for a far more fundamental reason. For her sanity—if nothing else—she needed time to think. And when Nick touched her, she leaped into pure sensation, unable to form a coherent thought.

"You wanted to know about my ex-husband," she gasped as his fingers slid beneath the hem of her shorts.

"I don't want to upset you."

"Oh…it's all right," she said hastily. "I stayed because marriage is important and serious and you don't just quit, you try to make it work."

"I'm glad to hear that. But what went wrong?"

Emily hesitated. "Uh…his biggest mistake. There was one thing I wouldn't take from Kevin, and when he tried it, I went out the door in a hurry."

At the sudden, dangerous stillness in Nick's body, Emily glanced up and saw his face had turned dark with anger.

"He hit you, didn't he?"

"*Tried*, Nick. He tried. But he was drunk at the time, and I can move pretty quick when I'm not pregnant."

Some of Nick's tension eased and he gently caressed her face. "You move great, *especially* pregnant," he corrected.

Sensual memories swept through Emily, and she snuggled closer. His skin was warm, stretched tautly over hard muscles and tendons, the result of a lifetime of hard work.

Nick didn't stand by idly and let other people sweat. When he devised a solution for an engineering problem, he stuck his hands in and toiled along with everyone else. She'd heard about it...the way he made everyone laugh and believe they could accomplish the impossible. She'd never completely appreciated that remarkable quality in him before. Or a lot of his remarkable qualities.

A small, happy smile curved her lips.

"Ah...the way you smile, Angel," Nick breathed, kissing her forehead, her cheeks, the lashes drifting over her eyes. "You make me forget everything."

"Oh?" Her eyes popped open and she grinned. "Still blaming me for your amnesia, I see."

"I didn't—"

"Oh yes, you did. That first day at the hospital."

"Then I apologize."

"You're forgiven." Extending a finger, Emily stroked the dark hair on Nick's chest. She'd been wary about touching him too much during their lovemaking. But she wanted to...she wanted to touch him the way he'd touched her. Totally. Completely. Holding nothing back. Giving everything. Hot and generous like the sun.

Yet no matter how hard she tried, she couldn't forget that every touch, every stroke, every intimate word might take her closer to the time when he'd remember everything and be horrified by the events of the past few days.

Suddenly a terrible thought occurred to her...what if he decided he had to stay with her because of what had happened between them? A misplaced sense of obligation?

Lord. Emily gulped down a wave of nausea. That would be even worse than him being angry or amused. They had an agreement about the baby. Clearly defined responsibilities. She didn't want Nick thinking she'd changed her mind and wanted more.

His dark gaze captured hers. "Angel..."

All at once Nick's stomach grumbled. *Loudly.* Despite her inner turmoil, Emily laughed.

"Gee, that was romantic," he drawled. "Anything else I can do to get you in the mood?"

"No. I'd better fix something to eat. A nice brunch. What kind of proper wife lets her husband collapse from hunger?"

Nick tapped her nose and chuckled. "Angel, honey, you're a fabulous wife, but don't give me that woman-cooking-for-her-man routine. You don't go for the traditional role stuff."

"Hey, I cook for you a lot," she protested.

"Yeah...and a whole lot more." His voice dropped into a husky whisper.

He rose easily to his feet, still holding her in his arms, and Emily blinked. Sometimes she couldn't believe his strength. "You seem to think I can't walk," she felt obliged to point out as he carried her to the kitchen.

"I know you can walk." Nick gave her a last, lingering kiss before letting her slide down the length of his body. "But this way, I can hold you longer."

When he was gone, Emily leaned over the butcher block counter and drew a series of fast, deep breaths. If pregnancy made a woman this insatiable, no wonder there was a population problem in the world.

"Control," she mumbled. "I need a little control."

So what if Nick was the sexiest, most thoughtful, in-

ventive lover alive. She could live without sex if she had
to.

Right?

Groaning, Emily dragged herself to the refrigerator
and stuck her head inside. The cold air didn't help. Nei-
ther did the scent of strawberries. Nick had devised some
very interesting things to do with strawberries. Her knees
wobbled at the memory.

"I'm out of my mind," she said as GeeZee darted
into the room and began a frantic dance about her feet.
"Just a minute," she ordered. "And get out of the way.
I happen to know you're not starving." But she was
grateful for the distraction. It made her think less
about…well…*strawberries.*

And Nick.

"Mooorrouw." The raucous cry pierced the air and
was followed by a second howl, even louder.

"Are you killing him?" Nick called.

The question filtered down from the second floor, and
she hoped he was up there putting on some clothes. A
fully dressed Nick was tempting enough—she didn't
need him any other way.

"No," she called back. "But I might if he trips me."

Three seconds later Nick charged into the kitchen.
He'd put on a pair of jeans, but they were unbuttoned
at the waist. He scooped GeeZee up, swearing at the
feline. GeeZee just hung in his arms and purred.

"It's not that bad," Emily protested, startled by
Nick's vehemence. "He just wants to eat."

"I'll grind him into hamburger if he makes you fall."

Emily rolled her eyes and took her cat from him. She
scratched GeeZee under the chin. "Men. You're all
alike—grumpy when you're hungry. Leave me alone so
I can get something done."

"Put him down, he's too heavy," Nick said automatically.

"Go," Emily ordered, but she softened it with a pert smile. "Don't worry, he isn't a problem. He just wants food. He usually gets to eat a lot earlier."

"And the thorn in my paw is caused by something else?" The fierce expression in his face faded, and he reached out to pet GeeZee, his fingers carefully brushing across her breasts in the process.

"Nick," she moaned.

"I know, I know. I have all the subtlety of a steamroller." His gaze moved across her slowly, almost tangibly, like a silent caress.

"You're not so bad."

"It's the kid in the candy store syndrome."

Emily leaned into him briefly, warmly...and bit her tongue to stay quiet. Not because it had been so long since she'd been intimate with a man. And not because of the definite feminine ache between her legs. But because it seemed important to act like a normal wife, accustomed to her husband's attentions.

Reality, not sensual fantasy.

A hastily constructed imitation marriage to give Nick what Paige called a "safety zone." Unfortunately that safety zone wasn't safe at all, not to her heart or their friendship.

Nick stepped back. "I'll be back," he said gruffly and walked out.

"Meooowww," demanded GeeZee.

Emily hugged the enormous feline and dropped him on the floor. "Rotten cat," she said fondly. She opened a can of food and filled GeeZee's bowl. "There. Don't blame me if you explode from overeating."

* * *

Nick bounded down the staircase again, buttoning his shirt and certain he'd never felt better or more energized in his life. Marriage was great. And marriage to Emily was especially great.

He'd spotted the mailman coming up the street, so he scooped up the pile of outgoing letters Emily had left by the door.

Hmm...bills.

Obviously. It was almost the end of the month, and Emily was the type to pay promptly. Curiously he flipped through them, hoping something might trigger a memory. But it was dry stuff.

A couple of mortgage companies.

Telephone—they probably had a terrific bill if he spent so much time away.

A property management company in Seattle.

Power.

A strange prickling sensation struck Nick, and he rubbed his neck. *Property management?* He flipped back to that envelope.

Two mortgage companies, *and* property management?

It seemed odd, so he opened the envelope, quashing a stab of guilt. After all, he was entitled to know the facts of his life. Inside he found a check attached to a piece of paper with his name and an apartment number written on it.

"How hungry are you?" Emily called from the back of the house.

The corner of the check crumpled in his hand. "Coffee and toast will be fine."

"Just toast? You must want more than that. I'll fix a chili omelet. You always liked them."

"Whatever." Nick stuffed the check and torn envelope into his back pocket and took the remainder out to the mailbox.

The meal was quiet. Too quiet. Emily kept giving him worried glances, especially the times his fork grated on the plate with unnecessary force. "Is something wrong?" she asked finally.

"Isn't that my line?"

His harsh tone widened her eyes.

Breathing deeply, Nick tried to control his doubts. After all, he could be overreacting. There might be a perfectly reasonable explanation for the check and the apartment...for everything. Just like the wedding pictures. "Sorry," he muttered.

Emily nodded, still looking worried. He watched as she ran her finger across the condensation gathering on her glass of milk.

Milk and orange juice, whole wheat toast and a poached egg. No coffee. A healthy brunch for an expectant mother. An omelet for dad. Everything seemed normal, but his tasty omelet sat on his stomach like a lead weight.

"Never mind me, Angel," he murmured, forcing a smile. "It just gets frustrating, not being able to remember. Kind of creeps up unexpectedly."

"I see."

"And you're so independent. You don't let me do much for you." Nick heard the anger and frustration creeping back into his voice, so he tried to think of something pleasant. Except the most pleasant thing he could think about was Emily.

"I don't mean to be difficult," she said hesitantly. "But that's the way I am. And...and with you gone a lot, it's best that I can manage things by myself. Isn't it?"

Nick thought about the envelope in his pocket. Gone? Was he really "gone," or spending time in Seattle? Could they be separated so soon after getting married? And what about Carmen? A name and a number on a matchbook.

He had to find out. He had to understand.

While Emily cleaned the kitchen, he hurried to the bedroom and looked up the number of the management company. Breathing deeply, he lifted the receiver and dialed.

"Howard and Wilcox Management Company. May I help you?" a young woman answered on the second ring.

"Yes, this is Nicholas Carleton—"

"Hi, sweetie." The voice changed from efficient to flirtatious. "You back in town?"

"Yeah. I just wondered if you've received the rent check on my apartment."

"Haven't seen it, sweetie, but we got the renewal on the lease. I'll watch for the check and let you know if it doesn't show."

"Er...thanks. I have to go now."

He hastily disconnected. *Sweetie?* That was awful. And whoever that woman might be, she didn't sound like she knew he was married. Was that Carmen? Surely not. The phone number on the matchbook was a foreign exchange, not domestic.

Sighing, Nick went into the half-finished nursery, tension snaking along his nerves. He glared at the cans of paint and other equipment. With each swipe of the roller, he'd envisioned Emily sitting in a rocking chair, nursing their baby. He'd imagined ruffles and lace and a little girl's smile that looked just like her mother.

And later...

Maybe they'd have another child. A boy he could play catch with in the woodsy backyard, or another daughter to protect and adore. *A family.*

Yet all of that might never happen.

With deceptive calm, Nick lifted a tarp over the baby furniture he'd assembled. He carefully put masking tape around the windows and on the wall along the molding before opening the white enamel paint.

Emily paused at the door several times, but he didn't turn around and he didn't say anything. It wouldn't help to lose his temper and say things he'd rather not say. They could discuss the apartment and their marriage after he cooled down.

Calm.

Rational.

No shouting.

He focused on the paintbrush as though his life depended on the even strokes. Emily had already made curtains, so he would install the brackets next.

Two hours later Emily stopped at the door again. "Please, tell me what's wrong."

Nick looked at her and wished he could just keep looking and not questioning. He wished he could go back to the moment before he'd seen the envelope. He wished he'd never checked the mail, or even thought of doing anything but loving Emily.

What kind of husband kept a wife in one town and an apartment in another?

And what kind of wife paid for that apartment when her husband had amnesia?

It sounded like a marriage on the edge of disaster.

Grimly Nick pulled the check from his pocket. "I decided to take the mail out for pickup. Look what I found."

Emily took the small piece of paper without a word.

"Angel...why the hell do I have an apartment in Seattle?"

She bit the corner of her lip. "You...well, you had a lease agreement. It hasn't run out yet."

"Try again. I called the company. They just got the renewal papers."

"You called?"

"What did you expect? Nothing makes sense—not even us."

If he hadn't been so miserable for himself, he'd have felt miserable for Emily. She looked sick. He was angry and sorry and confused. He wanted to comfort and rage at her, all at the same time.

"I know it seems strange," she said slowly.

Nick clenched his jaw against a savage, sarcastic remark. "Yes?"

Emily fidgeted with the hem of her T-shirt. "Your schedule is unpredictable. You fly in and out in the middle of the night a lot, so it's easier to stay in the city than catch a ferry and come all the way back to Crockett."

"Oh? Why not a hotel then? It would cost a lot less and we could have subleased the apartment." Nick watched her, wanting to be convinced. But a web of half-truths and uneasy silences entangled him.

"Well...you've had that place for quite a while—a long time before we got married. You're comfortable there and you don't have to bother with registration or anything. We talked about giving it up at the end of the lease, though we hadn't actually made a decision. You didn't tell me you'd decided to keep it, after all. Not that it's a problem," she added hastily.

Logical. Annoying. Emily's explanation sounded

valid. He had a vague impression of the time needed to drive from the airport, wait for a ferry, then drive to Crockett. Keeping an apartment in the city seemed expensive but convenient.

Yeah...too damned convenient.

What he had to discover is which one of them it "convenienced" the most.

If it was his stupidity, carrying on like a bachelor when he had a wife and child on the way, then he'd curse himself for acting ten kinds of fool and pray it wasn't too late to fix things.

If it was Emily....

The knot in Nick's stomach tightened. Emily belonged to him. She *had* to belong to him. And no matter what the cost, he feared he would accept any compromise to keep her. But first he needed to know which devil he was facing.

"Maybe you wanted me to keep my apartment in case our marriage didn't work out," he suggested in a low, hard voice.

"That's ridiculous," Emily scoffed.

"Really? I seem to be a temporary fixture, dropping into your life occasionally, but spending most of it in some other damned country, doing things separately and only stopping here to get my laundry done."

"When you remember, you'll understand," she said, probably for the hundredth time since he'd awakened in the hospital. She sounded desperate and guilty, and ironically...truthful.

"Things don't add up. We have to talk about this, Angel. *Now,* not later."

Angel. His pet name for her echoed in Emily's mind.

She tried to control her shaking. All along Nick had been suspicious and questioning of their relationship. He worried they were having marital problems. If she told him now...it might be all right. He might be relieved to find out there weren't any real commitments to be concerned about.

Or maybe not.

And she wouldn't be "Angel" anymore.

He wouldn't be treating her like the most wonderful, precious woman in the universe. He'd stop being protective and loving and so sweetly sensual. He might even think she'd broken their agreement about the baby.

Of course, she didn't *need* him to protect her or make her feel special, but it was nice.

Nice?

Emily shook her head. Who was she kidding? In the past few days she'd learned more about Nick than she had in all the years of their friendship. *Nice* didn't cut it.

Are you sure you want the old Nick back?

Yes.

No.

She wasn't sure about anything anymore. All the certainties of her life had vanished, lost in the hungry, passionate gaze of a man who knew her better than anyone, yet didn't remember. The same, but different.

Nick gently cupped her chin. "You have to talk to me."

"I don't know what to say." Emily flicked her tongue across her lips. "We're married. We're having a baby. It's just a little confused right now."

"Confused, huh? What part would that be?"

She smiled weakly. "Every part."

"At least we agree about that."

"We agree about a lot of things. I didn't lie about loving you, Nick. I've always loved you."

"Do you? Or did you want a baby so badly, you fooled yourself into believing you cared for me?" He said it so softly that it took a moment for the words to sink in.

"What?"

"Angel, I'd have to be blind not to see how important this pregnancy is to you."

"Of course it's important!"

"So...maybe you married me just to have the baby."

Emily's mouth opened and closed like an astonished fish. This was absurd. Absolutely the most absurd, unbelievable mess two people could find themselves in.

Of course she'd married him for the baby.

Nick...the *real* Nick, knew all about it. Hell, it was *his* idea! *He'd* insisted on the marriage. *He'd* insisted on donating the sperm for the baby. *He'd* been determined to prevent her from doing something so flagrantly unconventional as going to a sperm bank.

It was *his* fault.

Now here she was, pregnant with *his* baby, getting accused of the truth.

Life wasn't fair.

It wasn't even close. She scowled. If the real Nick was standing there, she'd poke a finger at his chest and tell him where to get off. But she'd promised Paige she wouldn't tell him the facts of their marriage, not without talking to her first.

And right now, talking to someone else sounded like a great idea. Her "marriage" was out of control.

"I have to go out for a while." Emily began backing out of the room.

"Out?" Nick stared at her incredulously. "You can't solve problems by running away."

Her teeth gritted at the implication of cowardice. *No*

one had ever accused her of being a coward, not even when she'd left Kevin. "I'm not running away."

"Looks like it to me."

"Well it isn't. I just need to be alone so I can think."

"You said marriage was important to you. I want to believe that, Angel. I really do. Whatever is wrong, we'll work it out."

Sincerity blazed in his brown eyes, and she didn't know whether to laugh or cry. Everything was so mixed-up.

Her feelings.

Nick's feelings.

Yet Nick only thought he cared for her because of the amnesia. It would be the same for any man who'd awakened with a blank memory, needing a foundation to stand upon.

Emily knew that wonderful, loving husbands and fathers existed in the male population. She even accepted that dedicated bachelors could turn into those loving husbands and fathers…she just didn't expect Nick to do it for her. They'd known each other for too long.

It would end when he got his memory back. Everything. Their friendship. Their so-called marriage. She'd never see this side of him again—the tender, passionate man who made her feel things she'd never felt before.

Frustrated tears overtook her impulse to laugh.

This wasn't funny in the slightest. It was infuriating, impossible and completely unnerving. But not funny.

"I'll see you later," she muttered.

And fled.

Chapter Eight

"He says I married him for the baby!"

Paige twirled a pen between her fingers. "You—"

"Can you believe it?" Emily paced back and forth in the small office and threw out her arms. "I married him for the baby…like some sort of rapacious, manipulative, baby-hungry woman without a conscience."

The physician leaned back in her desk chair and crossed her arms. "That's what—"

"Imagine, I 'fooled' myself into thinking I loved him," Emily growled. She glared at an innocent seagull sitting outside the window. "He practically said I'm a weak-minded idiot who would do anything to have a child."

Paige pressed her lips together.

"Ugh. Nick has come up with some nonsense in the past, but this is the worst. And it wasn't even one of his jokes, he was dead serious."

Emily put her hand over her round stomach and stroked it thoughtfully.

"At least...I don't think it was a joke," she said. "He can be pretty outrageous sometimes, but I'd swear he meant every word. What do you think?"

Paige lifted an eyebrow.

"I guess it doesn't matter," Emily muttered. "Either way, it's horrid of him. But to sit there and calmly tell me I just married him for the baby!"

"You *did* marry him for the baby," her friend exclaimed, exasperated.

"I know that, but the baby is *my* responsibility. This whole thing about donating the sperm was *Nick's* idea— he insisted, he just doesn't remember right now. Then to say something so awful after last night. I could scream."

"Last night?"

The question brought Emily up short and her face turned warm.

Last night.

Great. She should have kept her mouth shut. But Paige was a doctor, so she was professionally obligated to keep the whole thing confidential. Right?

"You're not going to tell anyone about this, are you?" she asked suspiciously. "I mean, Nick wouldn't appreciate everyone knowing our personal business."

Paige waited a moment then rocked forward and put her hands on the desk.

"Not that I care," Emily muttered. "He deserves what he gets. But this is a private conversation. And we're in your office," she pointed out. "So technically you're seeing me as the wife of a patient, not as a friend."

"You call this a conversation?"

Emily glowered. "Okay, I'm sorry. Help me. Say something constructive."

"All right." Paige tossed her pen down. "Based on your comment about 'last night,' I'd guess your relationship with Nick has changed radically. Also, since you feel betrayed by his accusations, I think you enjoyed yourself."

Enjoyed? Whoa. Now there was an understatement.

Her friend looked at her critically and said, "Like I told you before, I think it's about time."

"Was that a professional or personal observation?" Emily dropped into a comfortable chair and put her feet up. "And I don't feel betrayed," she denied quickly. "I'm angry, that's all. It's a very natural emotion."

"Sure. Look, if you had your choice, would you take Nick the way he is now?"

Emily moaned. "Any woman would take him. You wouldn't believe how loving and protective he's been. This morning I joked about GeeZee tripping me, and Nick charged into the kitchen like I'd screamed bloody murder."

"He's right, you should be careful not to fall in your condition," Paige murmured, ever the doctor.

"That isn't the point. He worries about everything. What I do. What I lift. What I eat. Well...actually, that kind of drives me crazy, but it's sweet."

"Don't knock it. Not every pregnant woman is so lucky. Besides, maybe Nick really loves you."

"He'd treat a total stranger the same way," Emily retorted. "He *thinks* we're in love, so he's acting the part of a loving husband."

"But—"

"*Acting.* It isn't real."

Paige looked at her. "But if it was...?"

Emily shook her head. She couldn't let herself hope that a normal marriage was possible, because it wasn't.

"I can't steal Nick's life from him, and I certainly can't take the anxiety of wondering when he'll open his eyes and remember this whole thing isn't real. He'll be horrified...not to mention utterly embarrassed."

"Hmm."

"And you know how men are. They hate being embarrassed."

Paige smiled and didn't say anything.

"Never mind. The important thing is for Nick to get his memory back," Emily said resolutely. "I have to tell him the truth."

Emily lifted grocery bags from the back of the Blazer and balanced them on her hip. Acting on Paige's advice, she'd delayed coming home to give Nick some time for reflection. She'd needed the time as well, yet it seemed cowardly.

"I'm not a coward," she muttered, emphasizing her words by kicking one of the Blazer's tires.

They'd decided to tell him about the marriage and artificial insemination. If that didn't work, Paige would set up some alternative treatments. Emily hoped it wouldn't be necessary; she didn't think she could survive much more turmoil.

It would be bad enough telling Nick the truth and losing the magic of the past few days. It might not have been real, but it had been wonderful, just the same.

"Angel?" Nick opened the front door as she walked up the steps. "Where have you been? I was worried about you." He took the bags of groceries and gave her a kiss. "I think it's going to rain."

Emily blinked and gave the sky a cursory glance. Clouds had gathered, obscuring the sun, and gusts of wind ruffled the trees. A summer rainstorm was brewing, yet the air still conveyed a muggy discomfort. "I...I went shopping."

"I see that." He smiled...a warm, sexy, melting smile. "Come inside. You look tired."

She blinked again. It felt like "The Twilight Zone." She'd left an accusing, angry man and returned to a tender, loving husband.

"I have to talk to you," Emily said, stepping into the cool interior of the house. She was distracted by the flowers filling the living room. Roses. Daisies. Daffodils. Irises. Every color imaginable, sending out a rich mixture of scents.

She followed Nick into the kitchen and saw the same bright display of flowers everywhere she looked. "Uh...where did these come from?"

Nick dropped the bags on the table and turned around. "The florist fairy. We can talk later. Why don't you take a nice long bath to relax, while I arrange dinner?"

"I'm fine. But we—"

Without a word he pulled her to him for another kiss, this time with plenty of tongue action. Emily was breathless and shaky before it ended.

"Nick?"

"I knew it," he said, in a vaguely satisfied voice. "Come upstairs. I have something to show you."

Still reeling, she obediently followed him up the staircase. Nick was dangerous. Men—especially old friends—shouldn't be able to kiss like that. It wasn't fair. It turned sensible women into blithering dolts.

They stopped at the door of the nursery and he pointed, "Ta-da! See, Angel? Isn't it great?"

A beautiful bentwood rocking chair sat in the middle of the finished nursery. The wood was golden and polished and looked perfect in the cheery yellow room.

"We didn't have a rocking chair," said Nick. He gazed at it proudly. "And I thought we needed one with the baby coming, and all."

"Where...how did you get it here?" Emily asked flustered. She'd taken the Blazer when she'd gone to see Paige, and she didn't think a rocking chair would fit in the front seat of Nick's Porsche.

He grinned. "The phone book. I called up a local furniture store and offered a bonus if they'd deliver it immediately. They brought three out for me to choose from."

Nick had gotten her a rocking chair. A perfect rocking chair. A little awed, Emily sat down and rubbed the smooth arms. The chair was comfortable and roomy for holding babies. She couldn't have picked a better one herself.

"Do you like it, Angel?"

A tear slid down her cheek. "It's wonderful."

"Hey, what's this about?" His thumb, hard with calluses, gently brushed the tear away.

"Hormones," she said. "Pregnant women cry a lot. We're entitled."

Nick knelt by the chair and rubbed her stomach. "She's moving," he whispered, and for an instant they both focused on the flutters in Emily's womb. "What does it feel like?" he asked, his face intent and wildly curious.

Tendrils of sensation spread from his touch and Emily couldn't help putting her hands over his. "Like...butterfly wings."

"It's amazing."

The wonder in Nick's eyes filled her heart with aching tenderness. "Yes."

"I read about it—she's already got fingers and toes

and everything," he said, his hand still snugly cupping her tummy. "Even though she's so small. Can you believe that?"

Emily leaned back, wishing she could cling to this brief, tranquil moment. But she had to tell him. Just because Nick had decided to ignore their argument, it didn't change anything.

"About this afternoon," she murmured. "I want to explain."

"No," Nick said quickly. "I'm sorry. I don't know what got into me."

"But—"

"Shh, Angel. It's in the past. I want us to be together." The solemn strength of his words sent a twinge of guilt through Emily.

"We have to discuss some things."

"It was a silly spat and we don't have to bring it up ever again." His eyes were warm with humor, but determination lurked in their brown depths.

"Nick, we *really* have to—"

"Aw…come on, Angel," he protested. "It's natural for couples to quarrel sometimes. It just happens. I'll bet you wanted to wring my neck for being so foolish."

Among other things.

She gazed at him doubtfully. "You're not still mad about the apartment?"

"Only for acting like a jerk." He laughed. "You must have thought I'd lost my mind, questioning something I didn't know anything about. But I do think we should give up the lease. It's too much money for a convenience, and I plan to change my work schedule, anyway."

Emily swallowed. "Change it?"

"Of course. I can't leave you and the baby alone so much. I want to be here."

"You do?" She wondered if there was an earthquake shaking the house, or if it was just her personal world trembling on its foundation.

"Absolutely. Now, you have a nice long bath." Nick kissed her throat, his breath fanning seductively across her skin. "And forget about that nonsense. I have."

With startling speed and grace for a tall man, he rose to his feet and strode out of the room. Emily grasped the arms of the rocking chair. Maybe she'd fallen down a rabbit hole. She certainly *felt* like Alice in Wonderland. Confused and bemused.

She turned her head and saw that yellow roses filled the bassinet. He'd spent a fortune on flowers. And though she was still baffled, she got up and checked the bedroom.

Yup. Flowers there, too. And the bathroom was lush with ferns and calla lilies, complementing the green and white decor.

It was romantic.

And extravagant.

You have to tell him the truth.

"I will...when the time is right," Emily told her pesky conscience. "But he's not upset anymore."

You just want another night.

Undisputable. She wanted another night. Another romantic, passionate night to remember when Nick was back in Seattle, either cursing her name or laughing his head off. It wouldn't make any difference. The damage was done. She couldn't take back the intimacy they'd already shared.

Resigned, she collected her robe and sexiest dress from the closet. She picked out a silk bra and panties and an expensive French perfume Nick had brought back from one of his trips. She'd dab some on strategic places. He'd like that.

But she came to a dead stop at the sight of herself in the dresser mirror. Sexy? Perfume on strategic places? Who was she kidding?

Emily turned from side to side. No dress or perfume could hide the fact she was nearly five months pregnant. And if she went downstairs dressed like a vamp, it would be an obvious invitation. So...she shouldn't look too eager.

Actually, she shouldn't look eager at all.

She should try to look *very* pregnant and *very* inaccessible. While she didn't believe there was any hope of saving her friendship with Nick, she had to try.

And she should try to tell him the truth if the right opportunity presented itself, so he wouldn't think she'd been taking advantage of the situation.

The corners of her mouth turned down as she discarded the sexy dress in favor of a long-sleeved jersey blouse and skirt. The soft fabric would mold around her tummy, leaving nothing to the imagination. Each ounce she'd gained in those five months would be faithfully revealed.

Her niggling conscience reminded her that Nick seemed to enjoy seeing her body carrying his baby. Naturally *his* was the operative word. She was carrying *his* baby, which stroked *his* ego and made *him* possessive. But it wouldn't last after his memory returned. The real Nick was barely interested in being a weekend father.

"Stop it," she muttered.

Sighing, Emily locked the bathroom door and wiggled out of her shorts and T-shirt. She didn't bother looking in the mirror again.

It would just depress her.

* * *

As the sound of rushing water and whirlpool jets filled the house, Nick grinned in relief. He didn't want to discuss their argument, though he felt guilty for deceiving her.

Phew.

Who could have thought a case of amnesia would change things so much? Who'd have thought that little Emily Carmichael would turn out to be the sexiest woman on seven continents? And why hadn't he realized it before?

He'd seen her in a whole new way, and she'd been forced to see him differently as well. And her response wasn't faked. Amnesia or not, she wouldn't have made love with him unless some genuine emotion existed.

Nick shook his head. He liked what was happening, though he was confused by it, too. And he didn't have any intention of letting things come to a screeching halt before he figured it out. It was a risky choice, but Emily was so obstinate, she wouldn't let things continue if she found out he'd gotten his memory back.

Hell, he *knew* Emily.

They'd made an agreement about the baby and she would stick to that agreement if it killed her. She would try to pretend nothing had happened and send him back to Seattle, or else she'd get so embarrassed she'd kick him back to South America.

Nothing doing.

But her independence worried him. Emily wanted to do everything on her own. Sure…she was willing to let him fix the plumbing, since she could just as easily call a repairman and they both knew it. But she didn't turn to anyone for the personal things.

Not to her family.

Not to him.

A small frown creased Nick's forehead. Emily hadn't even confided about wanting the baby until she'd set an appointment with a fertility specialist. And he'd had an awful time convincing her to accept him as a sperm donor.

We'll have to work on that, he thought. He didn't want to subvert her independence, he just wanted her to trust him.

Whistling softly, he set a table on the screened back porch. He couldn't do things that fancy, but he knew enough to put flowers and candles out, and *not* to use paper plates and plastic forks.

Nick waited until the bathwater began draining from the tub, then called their favorite Greek restaurant with an order, followed by a second call to alert the "delivery" service when the food would be ready.

A few minutes later he heard Emily call his name.

"Out here. On the porch," he said, lighting the last candle. The evening sky had grown so dark from the approaching storm that the candles weren't just a romantic detail, but a necessity.

"Uh...what's this?"

"A candlelight dinner, of course."

Nick turned around and couldn't keep from smiling. Emily's "don't touch" outfit made him want to touch even more. The clinging material covered her arms, but it also clung to her breasts and the rich promise of her stomach. And her golden hair was pinned in an elegant knot at the back of head, instead of flowing free. It begged for release.

His Angel.

Funny. Nick thought about the first time he'd seen

Emily. It had been Christmas, but the holly and bright decorations just made the bleakness of another foster home seem worse by comparison. Then Gabe had dragged him into the Carmichael household, filled with the scents of holiday baking and the warmth of a loving family. He'd been welcomed without a second thought.

And Emily had been there. Delicate and sweet and pretty as an angel. He'd never seen anything so wonderful, so he'd reacted with the typical gaucheness of an eleven-year-old boy, boggled by his first crush...he'd teased her unmercifully.

Hell, he hadn't even realized it was a crush. He'd just wanted her to notice him. He *still* wanted her to notice him. Perhaps that explained why he'd teased her so much over the years.

"What are you grinning about?" Emily asked suspiciously.

It was on the tip of his tongue to tell her, but he remembered in time that he had "amnesia."

"You," he murmured, sliding his hand around the back of her neck and pulling her close. "You look great, Angel."

"I..." Whatever she intended to say got smothered in a kiss.

"Er...I ordered some food from a Greek restaurant," Nick said, releasing her slowly. "I tried not to get anything too weird."

"I love Greek."

I know. "Good. Lucky guess."

"Yeah." Emily glanced around the porch. Flowers were tucked everywhere—cut flowers and pots spilling lobelia and petunias over the edge, freesias—illuminated by the flickering light from dozens of candles. "It's lovely," she said breathlessly. "You went to a lot of trouble."

He stroked her back. "We'll go inside if it gets too cool. You mustn't get chilled."

Emily wrinkled her nose. Like Paige said, some women weren't fortunate enough to have a protective husband. Of course, some women had normal husbands who'd actually intended to *be* a husband.

"I'm fine," she said. "I've got long sleeves, and I get too warm, especially being pregnant."

"That explains why I can't keep you covered up at night. You kept kicking the blankets off," Nick explained at her questioning expression.

He continued to rub her back, his handprint burning through the thin jersey of her blouse. Emily gritted her teeth and pretended to enjoy the caress. Well...she *did* enjoy it, she just couldn't let herself enjoy it too much.

The urgent clang of the doorbell distracted them both.

"Our food must be here," he murmured.

Emily followed Nick through the house, her eyes widening at the sight of flashing lights on the street outside. A police car was parked haphazardly at the curb.

"What's going on?" she asked.

"Darned if I know."

Hank McAllister thrust three large sacks into Nick's arms as he opened the door.

"Gotta go," Hank said hastily. "I just got a call about kids spray painting the water tower."

"Dumb." Nick shook his head. "They should have waited until it was dark. You shouldn't have any trouble catching them."

"Harrumph."

"Kind of reminds you of the old days, huh?" Nick called after the departing figure.

Hank grunted something unofficerlike.

"Thanks for the delivery," Nick said.

The cruiser peeled out and Emily sighed. "The neighbors are going to think this is a drug house or something."

She received a consoling smile.

"Never mind, Angel. We'll be Ozzie and Harriet Nelson from now on. The most boring couple on the block."

"Huh. Mrs. Pickering won't buy that. And what about that stuff about the old days? Do you remember something?" she asked hopefully.

Nick blissfully inhaled the fragrant steam lifting from the restaurant bags. "Hank said we were the Terror of Crockett, and I can't imagine a Terror of Crockett failing to paint the water tower."

"Twice," Emily said succinctly.

"Twice? Didn't we get it right the first time?"

"Yeah…that's why the city fathers made you paint it again."

"Well, our kids aren't going to do any of that wild stuff."

"With your genes?" she scoffed.

"Gee, that really hurts." He looked at her stomach significantly. "But I guess it's too late to do anything except pray."

Nick took the food into the kitchen and unpacked the various containers. From the look of things, he planned to eat Greek for the rest of the month. *Dolma, spanakopitas, moussaka*…a dozen different entrees with two salads and six enormous pieces of baklava, dripping honey and almonds between flaky layers of rich pastry.

"Isn't this excessive?" she asked dryly.

"I wanted to get something you liked. Besides, we

haven't eaten since this morning. That isn't healthy, especially since you're eating for two.''

"Two, not eighteen. And how did you get Hank to deliver this stuff when he's on duty?"

"Dinner break. We're lucky his emergency call wasn't for anything more serious than spray paint, or our meal would have been sidetracked into law enforcement." Nick broke off a chunk of baklava and waved it in front of her mouth. "Open up."

"Mmm." The sweet, rich flavor burst across her tongue. "I love this stuff."

The sensual warmth in Nick's smile sent tremors through Emily's stomach. He seemed different tonight. She couldn't quite define the difference, but it was definitely there. The beginning of awareness? A hint of knowledge that hadn't been there before? If he was about to remember, then it would best to tell him the truth before he figured things out on his own.

"Uh...Nick, there are some things you ought to know."

"Nothing that can't wait." He looked at her intently. "Right, Angel?"

She swallowed and said, "Right," at the same time her mind jeered at her, *chicken.*

"Go on and sit down. I'll get you some milk and bring the food out."

Nick watched Emily take small sips of milk between bites of baklava. She'd been unusually quiet all evening, and he knew she was searching for the right opportunity to tell him the truth about their marriage.

But hell, what was the truth? Things had changed. They couldn't go back to being just friends. He wanted her to keep seeing him as a man she desired.

He shifted uneasily in his chair. Emily was a sweet-heart—she was also the most stubborn woman imaginable. She'd made up her mind to have the baby by herself, and if he wasn't careful he could end up back in Seattle with nothing but polite visitation rights. Once that might have been enough, but not anymore.

The whisper of raindrops worked their way into the porch, promise of a torrent to come. He glanced at the ceiling, wondering if the repairs on the roof were enough to keep it from leaking.

"Yum." Emily licked her fingers and settled back. "I'll bet I gained ten pounds tonight. See my tummy? It's twice as big."

That won't work, Angel, Nick thought, silently laughing. He didn't care if she gained a hundred pounds, she'd still be beautiful. He shifted again, his body stirring as he watched her in the dancing candlelight.

No matter what she might think, he didn't regret their lovemaking. Except maybe the length of time it had taken to get her into bed...more than twenty-five years. God, he must have been blind.

"You're not that big," he said softly. "But in a couple of months we'll probably have to start getting creative."

Emily rubbed the back of her neck and her eyes blinked sleepily. "Creative?"

"Yeah. In bed."

She jerked upright and glared, suddenly wide-awake. "That isn't funny. We're not getting creative anything. It doesn't sound safe."

"Perfectly safe," he assured with a straight face. "And there are all sorts of gravity-defying positions we can try."

"Nick!" His name came out in a strangled, exasperated tone. "You're impossible."

Rising from the comfortable Adirondack chair, he crossed to her side of the table and knelt in front of her. "I'm just being an attentive husband," he murmured.

Slowly he pulled the pins from her hair, so it tumbled down in a golden stream across her breasts. He cupped her stomach, astounded and aroused by the resilient mound. How could he have been so foolish, trying to ignore her pregnancy?

That was *his* child, no matter how it had been conceived.

A smile tugged at Nick's mouth as he recalled his discomfort over the details. Sure...the doctor's office had been about as humiliating an experience as he'd ever experienced. But that was all over with. They'd make their next baby in the regular way.

"Should we go inside?" he asked. "It's cooler now with the rain." *And we can snuggle in bed. I'm really looking forward to winter, this year.*

"No," Emily said quickly. "It feels good. I've never liked the heat." She settled deeper into her chair, giving every indication of sitting there for the rest of the evening. "If you have something to do, go right ahead."

"Angel," Nick groaned. "You *know* what I want to do."

She bit her lip.

"It was all right last night, wasn't it?" he asked. "You weren't uncomfortable?"

"N-no. It was okay."

Okay?

Nick told himself that Emily was playing "hands off"—*not* trying to pulverize his ego. Anyway, ego crushing wasn't her style. She was strong and sweet and so damned special it turned him inside out.

It would be even better now that his memory had returned. He wouldn't have that niggling worry in the back of his blank mind, wondering what horrible things he might have done to drive her away from him.

Carmen?

A choked laugh rose from Nick's throat as he recalled the conversation he'd had just a week ago in the El Flamenco bar. They'd been relaxing after a tough job, and his friend, Raoul Molina, kept raving about the birth of his daughter...named Carmen, of course.

Reluctantly, then with increased excitement, Nick had shared his own approaching fatherhood. Raoul had written his phone number on the matchbook, making him promise to call the minute the baby was born.

Nick ran his hands up Emily's legs and felt her shiver. "Let's go upstairs," he coaxed.

"We...I..." She stuttered into silence and he could see conflicting emotions in her eyes. Apprehension, doubt, questions—but most of all, desire. He felt like a heel for pushing her, yet he truly believed they had a chance for a future together. They just needed a little time to make it possible.

"Angel?"

A quiet sigh breathed through her lips and Emily framed his face with her fingers. "Not upstairs," she whispered. "Right here. Right now."

Nick's chest expanded with tenderness and passion. He kissed the corner of her mouth. "The bed is better. You'll be more comfortable and it's warmer." He stroked her stomach again.

Emily's lips compressed and she wiggled up from the low-slung chair, perching on the edge. Everything he said or did was prefaced with a concern about the baby. Maybe this whole thing was based on a false sense of intimacy, brought on by amnesia and her pregnancy. It hurt, thinking that any woman might have provoked these feelings in Nick.

"I'm not fragile," she said, emphasizing her point by pushing at his chest and unbuttoning his shirt in the process. "I won't break if you touch me, and I don't have to be treated like an invalid."

She slid off the edge of the chair, landing over him. Her skirt had ridden up and she squirmed until she could sit astride his legs. His arousal strained the zipper of his jeans, pushing against her barely protected softness.

Well...maybe it wasn't just the pregnancy that attracted him. She wished she could make up her mind.

A raspy sound rose from Nick's throat.

She smiled, a small, fierce, satisfied smile. *Protective* might be okay sometimes, but not tonight. Tonight she needed to know it was just the two of them—without thought of babies or pretend marriages or amnesia or anything else.

"Angel...sweetheart, the porch isn't the most private place in the world," he muttered into her hair.

Emily lifted the bottom of her turtleneck shirt and pulled it over her head. The faint hiss of Nick's breath made her smile again. She arched her back and flung the garment aside.

"Private? Of course it's private." She pushed his own shirt over his shoulders. "There's nothing but trees and bushes and a fence. Just the great outdoors. No neighboring windows and spying eyes—not even a chance we'll be seen. And I don't want to wait."

The masculine heat thrusting against her thigh became even harder. "Hmm," she purred. "Imagine we're teenagers exploring the possibilities of life. We're going steady and we just got home from the prom,'' she said dreamily.

"Angel," Nick whispered, his gaze sliding over her hotly, "I *feel* like a teenager."

No you don't. Emily ran her fingers over the contours of his body, surrendering more of the emotional distance she'd tried to preserve. She loved the way he felt—like a man. Tough and strong, with eyes that had seen the world and still knew how to smile.

His fingers cupped her silk-covered breasts, his thumbs rotating her nipples into taut knots. Heat glittered through her body.

"We just got home from the prom?" Nick prompted.

"Uh...yeah." She wiggled closer. "It's past curfew and my dad is upstairs. He's sure going to be mad if he catches us. This goes *way* beyond necking."

"Necking?" he repeated thickly, unfastening the clasp on her bra. For a long moment she stared into his face, memorizing every nuance of passion and need reflected there.

"You know, old-fashioned fooling around. Want a 'hickey' you can brag to your friends about?" With sensual precision, her teeth tested the strength of his skin and the corded muscles of his shoulder.

"That isn't how you make a hickey," he said raggedly.

"Sorry." Emily licked the tiny mark left by her teeth. Nick shuddered and his finger dug into her hips. "Boy, is my father going to be sorry he trusted you," she drawled.

"Angel, your father was crazy if he *ever* trusted me," Nick muttered. "Or you."

"Does that mean you're going to break the rules?"

"What rules?"

"Nothing below the collarbone in the front, or below the waist in the back," Emily quoted, though the "rules" hadn't been a big problem for her as a teenager...not with Nick and her oldest brother around to make sure the boys were too terrified to try much touching.

A laugh rumbled through Nick. "I think we've already trashed those boundaries."

Holding her tightly, he shimmied backward. Emily gasped and clung to him, certain he planned on carrying her to the bedroom upstairs. "No," she said determinedly. "We're not going anywhere."

Nick murmured something that sounded like a reassurance, then grabbed the thick cushion from the chaise lounge. With a desperate groan he slung the pad onto the floor and rolled them both on top of it.

Chapter Nine

Nick curled around Emily on the narrow cushion, trying to get some control over his body. It wasn't easy. His mind kept saying be gentle, while his hands were busy discarding their remaining clothing. A sheen of sweat dampened his body as he struggled between concern for his wife and child, and the promise of sweet, oblivious pleasure.

He leaned over Emily and felt a drop of water land on his shoulder. Behind them a candle sizzled, extinguished by another drip.

"Angel, the roof's still leaking. We should...um..." His words ended in a low moan as she arched against him like a golden-haired cat—all languid and hot, but with a hidden purpose. And her hands...they touched him in ways he could only have imagined.

Well...it might be okay. The chaise lounge pad was pretty thick—one of the expensive kind, and he could balance his weight on his arms. Or they could try one of those more creative positions he'd teased her about.

The leaky roof was mostly an inconvenience, and it wasn't all *that* cold.

And it was erotic, the thought of making love on the porch with the candlelight glowing around them. Long, flickering glints of light and shadow caressed Emily's silken skin. They'd never had the fun of a courting couple. Perhaps she wanted that now...some of the carefree youth her first marriage had cheated her from enjoying.

Get to know Emily again. Let her get to know you. You might learn some things you didn't know before. Nick said a fervent thank you in his mind to Paige Wescott. She'd given him excellent advice.

"You look so serious."

"I am serious." He looked deeply into her eyes, the color of midnight velvet in the dusky light. "You can count on me, Angel."

You can count on me. Edgy guilt stirred inside of Emily. When Nick remembered, would he think he'd made a promise he had to keep?

She shook her head determinedly and ran the bare curve of her foot over his leg. It still seemed strange to be with him, naked and breathless with anticipation. And wonderful. But if she thought much about it she'd probably want to crawl under a rock. After all, this was *Nick.* Her buddy.

"You're making me crazy," he whispered.

Crazy? *Crazy* was nice. *Crazy* translated to unguarded passion.

Emily put her arms around Nick and stroked the play of muscles beneath his skin. Down the center of his back was a trail of moisture, and she followed its path with her fingers. As she burrowed against his chest, grazing him with the hard points of her breasts, his breathing turned into deep, heavy gasps.

"You like that?" she asked with seeming innocence.

"God, Angel, you have no idea."

He took her mouth, bending her neck over his forearm with the force of his kiss. Not gently arousing, but possessive and demanding. Dimly she recognized the unleashed passion in him. It should have frightened her, but it didn't. Just once, she wanted everything.

Nick caught her breasts and kneaded them with his strong hands. Emily moaned, her nails scoring his back. This time she didn't hesitate, she put her hands on his shoulders and pushed, letting him know she wanted the heat of his mouth suckling her.

He teased her at first, tickling the sensitive nipple with his tongue and breath. Just when she thought she couldn't stand waiting any longer, he drew upon the dusky tip with a fierce, tender pressure.

The shock of lightning and thunder in the dark sky couldn't compete with the fireworks inside the porch. Nick's powerful, aroused body slid between her legs, and she welcomed him, the tightening spiral of fulfillment beginning with his first intense thrust.

"Nick?" she pleaded raggedly, not even knowing what she wanted.

"I'm here, Angel," he said with a husky, masculine groan. "I told you. I'm not going anywhere without you."

And he didn't.

Emily yawned and stretched, sensing a pleasant sensual ache in her body. She wasn't accustomed to such demanding nighttime activity.

A smile drifted across her lips.

"Ah...what a smile, Angel," Nick's voice rumbled. "You look like a contented cat."

Emily rolled on her back and blinked at him sleepily. "You're up."

"I was up most of the night."

A faint blush warmed her cheeks, because she knew what *up* he was referring to, and it didn't have anything to do with getting out of bed. "Bragging?" she managed to ask tartly.

"No...just happy. I brought you some breakfast."

Nick nudged her hip with a tray, and she scooted to the middle of the bed, staring at his bare shoulders and the unsnapped waistband of his jeans.

Lord, he was delicious. A familiar, melting sensation poured through her veins. It was tempting...they could spend another day in bed and forget about the world.

No.

She couldn't delay telling him the truth any longer. She'd had her romantic night, but now it was over. *Really* over. She glanced out the window and saw the storm had blown through, leaving fresh-washed sunshine in its place. Yet the sound of lightning and thunder would always remind her of how it felt to have Nick in her arms...filling her with his strength and overwhelming passion.

Emily shifted restlessly.

Don't think about that.

She sat up, holding the sheet over her bare breasts.

Nick grinned. "Too late, Angel. I already know what they look like. Perfect...I might add."

Wrinkling her nose and smiling at the same time, Emily tucked the sheet more securely around her. "You don't have any modesty, Nicholas Carleton. You never did."

"Maybe...but at least I feed you." He dug a spoon into a pink concoction in a bowl and held it out.

"That isn't yogurt, is it?" she asked. "I can't do yogurt this early."

"Uh-uh. Häagen-Dazs raspberry sorbet. I...er... figured it would be easier on your tummy." He waved the spoon. "Open up."

Häagen-Dazs? For breakfast? Sinful indulgence. Emily tried not to let it weaken her resolve. She'd eat some sorbet, then tell him the truth. She couldn't put it off any longer, and it seemed impossible to find a "right time" for this type of revelation.

She opened her mouth, and the sweet, tangy flavor of raspberries flowed over her tongue.

Oh, dear.

Nick didn't know it, but he wasn't playing fair. She loved Häagen-Dazs.

Dropping her death grip on the sheet, she took the spoon from Nick and savored another mouthful. He grinned and tugged the sheet until it settled around her hips. Emily didn't really mind until a drop of the frozen dessert dripped from the spoon and landed on her chest.

"Yeow!" she yelped.

She looked down and saw the melting drop roll unerringly down her right breast and hover on her nipple. She couldn't help it, she giggled.

"Oops." Nick took the bowl and tray and put them on the bedside table. "It must some kind of weird chemical process because of the baby. You didn't get drunk eating Häagen-Dazs before getting pregnant."

Before?

The breath caught in Emily's throat. He'd remembered? A combination of fear and embarrassment twisted her stomach. She was sitting in front of him, absolutely naked, with the scent of their lovemaking still clinging to the sheets. She wanted to crawl under a rock. Or at least under the bed.

She swallowed. "Uh...Nick, I—"

Emily's eyes flew open as the rough velvet of his tongue swirled about her nipple. "Sorbet can't compete with this, Angel. You taste too good."

A terrible suspicion entered her mind. Though it was hard to ignore the tantalizing, sultry warmth of Nick's mouth on her breast, she thought furiously about the past evening.

Greek food. Every single one of her favorite dishes. Not even a near miss, out of a dozen choices.

A refusal to discuss the past, when he'd been so determined to learn the truth of their relationship during that ridiculous argument about the apartment and the baby.

Kind of reminds you of the old days. The days when Nick and Hank and Gabe had been the Terrors of Crockett and had painted the water tower.

No wonder he had seemed different—even more like his old self. *He'd remembered.* And not this morning...yesterday.

Her eyes narrowed dangerously. However illogical, she felt stupid and foolish and so damned furious she could scream.

"Nick?"

"Mmm." Nick shifted and she took the opportunity to give him a hard shove. He tumbled over the edge of the bed and she scrambled off the other side, angrily pulling the sheet from the mattress and wrapping it around herself like a sarong.

"What the hell?"

"Don't say anything," she hissed.

He looked at her warily.

"You snake...you manipulated me. How could you not tell me you'd gotten your memory back?"

Nick groaned.

"How could you touch me like that when you must have known what I was going through?" Bewildered and hurting, Emily stared at him. *How could you make love to me?*

Nick leaned forward and laid his hands flat on the mattress. "Let me explain."

"You don't have anything to explain. You're a despicable fraud. I agonized about saving our friendship, but you were willing to just trash it for another night of fooling around. Well, fine. You got what you wanted, now you can get out of my life. I hope you thought it was funny."

"It wasn't like that."

"Right."

"Right," he growled back. "You responded to me, Emily. You enjoyed it as much as I did. You can't deny that."

"I—" She glared, because she couldn't deny something so absolutely true. "It's just because I'm pregnant. It makes a woman more responsive, that's all. A biological response. It had nothing to do with you."

"Bull. You wanted this." Nick made a broad gesture encompassing the rumpled bed, and symbolically, the passion they'd shared. "You were with me every inch of the way. And it had nothing to do with you being pregnant. It was *us*, together. That kind of heat is damned rare, and I won't let you throw it away."

"It all comes down to sex." Emily grabbed his wallet from the dresser and flung it at him. "Get out."

"Angel, please listen."

Angel. She hadn't thought her heart could hurt more

than it already did, but new pain sliced through her, proving her wrong again.

"Don't call me that."

"Why not? You're an angel to me—you always have been." Nick's voice sounded sure and certain, but she didn't care. He'd fooled her once already. How could he do this to her?

"I'm not anything to you, Nick. Just a joke. Just another one of those silly women you charmed into bed. When it came right down to it, that's all I was worth to you."

His eyes darkened. "This is crazy. You're my wife, Emily. You're carrying my baby."

Emily slapped her forehead, then had to make a desperate lunge for the slippery sheet. "A marriage of convenience, remember? No actual commitment."

"For God's sake, Angel, listen to me."

"No."

Emily picked up his set of keys and flung them in his general direction. She missed. They sailed through an opening in the curtain, smacked the open windowsill and bounced into the yard below.

"Get out." He didn't move, so she stomped her bare foot. "I said to get out." Her voice rose on each word, tearing at her throat.

"This isn't accomplishing anything."

They stared at each, Emily's face white with pain and anger. She crossed her arms over her stomach and shivered. It was too much...the fighting and hurting and confusion.

Nick growled something indistinguishable and strode out of the room. Emily quickly dropped the sheet and gathered several armfuls of the clothing she'd collected from his apartment. They followed the keys.

"I don't care what you do, I'm not leaving," he shouted from outside. She peered through the curtains and saw him searching through the azaleas.

"Yes you are," Emily muttered. She had every right to kick him out of her house, and that's what she intended to do. Snatching her robe from the bathroom, she headed down the staircase. The dead bolt slid into place with a satisfying click and she leaned against the door for a second.

"Angel, let me in."

"Go away."

Unable to stop herself, Emily burst in tears. How could she have fallen in love with Nick after all these years? It wasn't possible.

Hormones, she thought hysterically. Her pregnancy hormones had turned her into a watering pot. She didn't really love him. In a few days everything would be all right. Her body would settle down and she wouldn't keep thinking such nonsense.

Except...her hormones felt an awful lot like a broken heart.

Nick leaned his forehead against the door. It was awful to hear Emily crying. It made him sick to his stomach. She almost never cried.

He'd really blown things. While he'd thought it was risky not to tell her, it had never occurred to him she'd feel so betrayed. Embarrassed maybe, and determined to return their relationship to its old footing, but not betrayed. He'd just wanted more time to work things out—to let her see how much he wanted to be a part of her life and that of their baby. Not a joke. Not a cheap manipulation for sex.

Just time.

He didn't understand women.

He and Emily were so perfect together. Why couldn't she see that?

Sighing, Nick looked up and saw Mrs. Pickering staring at him from down the block. He shrugged his shoulders and received a disapproving frown in return. She looked at his clothing scattered across the front yard and shook her head. Though he wanted to be annoyed with the old busybody, he couldn't really blame anyone but himself.

Each muffled sob from the house ripped through his heart, teaching him more of pain and regret than he'd ever known, even in his lonely childhood. Now he realized he'd been in love with Emily forever—or at least since she was eight and he was eleven and he'd pulled her hair for the first time.

"Cripes," Nick muttered. "I've been such an idiot." It had taken a blow to the head and a case of amnesia to finally knock some sense into him.

Getting his memory back hadn't been nearly so startling. Actually, getting his memory back had been funny. He'd howled with laughter when he'd recalled his accusations that Emily had "fooled" herself into loving him so she could have the baby. He'd even anticipated sharing the humor with her.

He'd forgotten that men and women looked at sex in different ways. And he couldn't even blame amnesia for the lapse.

Nick turned the keys in his hands, recognizing each one. His car, her car, apartment…house. Yeah, Emily couldn't really keep him out, not when he had keys that opened everything she owned. If only he could find the key to sharing her life. But at the moment she wasn't in any mood to listen, and she probably wouldn't believe him, anyway.

Well, too bad.

She was his wife. Somehow he *had* to make her listen.

Nick stood quietly for a few minutes, plans racing through his mind. First he'd call Paige Wescott and ask her to check on Emily. Then he'd go back to Seattle long enough to take care of his apartment.

Really take care of it.

He'd get them to tear up the new lease, or pay them off…whatever it took. By evening he planned to be homeless.

He knew Emily. She was too softhearted to turn away a homeless husband. Right?

Emily bent over the sink and splashed water into her face. She hated crying. It was irrational and didn't accomplish anything except to make your eyes red. At least she had the excuse of being pregnant.

She sniffed and put her hands over her stomach.

Paige had called—apparently Nick had told her about their argument. Emily hadn't felt like talking, so she'd said she was fine—a bald-faced lie—and gotten off the phone.

Emily sighed and wandered downstairs. She lay on the couch with GeeZee and watched afternoon shadows chase across the ceiling as the breeze ruffled the trees outside. If she had any sense, she'd go down to the shop and work.

Obviously she didn't have any sense. If she did, she never would have agreed to Nick's ridiculous plan in the first place.

Sperm donor?

Huh.

Marriage of convenience?

What a laugh.

Emily bent her knees and tapped her fingers on her rounded stomach. It was just so...so *intimate* now. So real. This was Nick's baby inside her body. And now that they'd made love, it seemed as though every part of her had been exposed.

Of course, it wasn't entirely his fault.

To a certain extent she could blame amnesia and hormones. But not for last night—not for the way he'd been willing to destroy their friendship.

Emily yawned, exhausted by the emotional turmoil of the past few days. Her eyes drooped as she curled onto her side. GeeZee purred like a big furry tranquilizer, and she gradually fell asleep, lulled by the comforting sound.

Shortly after six that evening Nick parked his Porsche 911 in the driveway and smiled with grim satisfaction. He'd have to get a family car. A big one. The Porsche might be fun for a bachelor, but it didn't carry much.

Fortunately—depending on the way you looked at things—he didn't own much. And undoubtedly Emily had moved a lot of his belongings to Crockett when he'd gotten amnesia.

Hesitantly Paige had explained why she'd insisted on Emily preserving the illusion of a "normal" marriage— it would have been too confusing to know the truth in the beginning.

Confusing?

"Lord." Nick shook his head. Confusing wasn't an adequate word. He recalled his alarm that first day in the hospital...the panic of not being able to remember his own name. And he remembered his feelings at the sight of Emily—beautiful and worried—with her gold hair tumbled around her shoulders.

Pride. Elation. *Lust.*

Thank God for the amnesia, or it might have taken another twenty-five years to realize how much he loved her.

Nick smiled and unfolded himself from the low seat of the car. With a generous use of the apartment garbage chute, he'd managed to fit everything into the passenger seat and front-loading trunk.

That wasn't the hard part. The hard part would be convincing Emily to give him…*them,* a chance.

It was dinnertime, so the neighborhood was quiet except for the ching-ching of a sprinkler in the next yard. On the porch he found the clothing he'd left on the lawn neatly stuffed into two duffel bags, next to a large box filled with personal items. Cross-country skis leaned drunkenly against the wall, and his tool box had been dropped so hard the wood beneath was dented.

When Emily did a job, she did it right.

From what he could tell, everything he'd kept in Crockett had been packed and discarded.

His lips compressed as he reached into the box and pulled out the envelope containing their marriage certificate. He glanced inside, relieved to find Emily hadn't destroyed the document. That certificate meant everything to him. He wanted it to mean everything to her.

Naturally, the door was locked. Nick pressed the doorbell and waited. He would use his keys as a last resort…if she hadn't gotten a locksmith in the meantime.

The curtains covering the large front window swayed, so he punched the ringer again and kept pushing it.

"I told you to go away," Emily finally shouted through the closed door.

"That was this morning."

"I don't care if it was ten years ago. We don't have anything to discuss."

"That isn't true. Let me in, Angel. I'm homeless. I had to forfeit a two-thousand-dollar security deposit to get them to tear up my lease."

"So? That's your problem. Sleep on the boat."

Damn. He'd forgotten *The Lazy Skipper* with its galley and head and sleeping compartments. "Gee, I'd sure hate to sink her. But I will if I have to. This is my home now, I'm staying."

"No, you're not."

"Come on, Angel," he pleaded. "This isn't getting us anywhere."

"No."

"Emily, be reasonable."

Nothing.

Nick lifted his fist and pounded on the door. "Talk to me, Angel. I'm not going away."

"If you don't leave I'm calling the police."

"Go ahead." He kept pounding the door and calling to her, and after several minutes three squad cars and a county sheriff pulled up, lights flashing.

Hank McAllister got out of the first vehicle, crossed his arms and leaned against the hood. He shook his head and grinned. "Need any help, Nick?"

"No..." He waved to his friend between blows to the door. "I'm doing fine."

"Okay. Just let us know."

A fire engine drove leisurely down the street and parked next to the sheriff's vehicle. From the corner of his eye, Nick saw the assorted officers put their heads together, but no one approached the house. He didn't think they were worried about the dangers of a domestic dispute—it looked more like a party.

"Emily, you don't understand. Let me explain about last night. I wasn't trying to hurt you."

"You've always been a practical joker. I'll bet you thought it was plenty fun tricking me like that."

The hurt and humiliation in her voice tore at Nick. "It wasn't a joke." He lowered his voice so their audience couldn't hear. "Ah...Angel, all those years of teasing—I just wanted you to pay attention to me. I still do."

"Sure."

"It's true. I was always Gabe's friend, the aggravating buddy you tolerated—never a member of the family. But at least I was *there*...a part of your life in some way. I hated it when you got married. I didn't understand why, but it killed me to see you with another man."

Silence.

He sighed and leaned against the doorframe, wishing there was a way of letting Emily see into his soul. He'd concealed that part of himself...the hungry boy who'd seen an angel, but had been afraid to ask for too much. And he couldn't stop being that boy, not without Emily.

"Try harder," one of the firemen called. "I've got ten bucks on you."

"Damn," Nick muttered. That's all he needed—a cheering section taking bets on the outcome. Emily's pride had been wounded enough by this mess. She didn't...*couldn't* know how much she meant to him.

"I've got twenty on Emily," Hank contributed.

"Swell." Nick looked at the solid door. "Angel?"

"Yes?"

Good. At least she was talking again.

"I didn't tell you I'd gotten my memory back because

I knew you'd push me away. You're so independent. You're determined to do everything on your own...especially the baby. I thought if we just had more time, we could work things out.''

"We don't have anything to work out. And what's wrong with me being independent?" she asked belligerently.

"Nothing. I know it sounds silly, but I want to be needed...to know you trust me. I want you to know that I'm here."

Inside the house Emily crossed her arms and glared. That was the stupidest thing she'd ever heard. Of course she knew Nick was there. The whole *world* knew he was there. Nicholas Carleton wasn't the sort of man you could ignore. And she'd been trying *really* hard.

"Please, Angel."

Emily scowled harder. He couldn't get around her with that pleading tone. She had some principles, after all.

"Are you still there?"

"Yes, and that's all a bunch of nonsense. I'm too independent? Huh. You're *always* here. You insist on doing all the work on the house, even though you grouse about it and drag your feet. Then if I take care of something while you're gone, you act like a hurt little boy. So I have to leave it until you get back."

"Exactly."

"Exactly what? That I'm dependent on you? I'm not."

"No. But at least you needed me for the little things."

Emily wiggled her foot. "Sheesh. That's the dumbest thing I've ever heard. We were friends, you dope. I even told you about my plans for the baby. You were the *only* one I told."

She could hear his sigh, even through the door. "Okay. So my subconscious was dumb—I didn't say it made sense."

"Go back to Seattle," she said. "You don't need me. I'll bet you've probably got a hundred girlfriends. And they must be a lot *thinner,* too."

"I don't care about thin."

"Sure. I used to have a waistline before you got me pregnant." She tugged at her maternity dress, then folded her arms over her tummy.

"Uh, Angel," Nick hesitated, and his voice lowered even more. "You wanted to get pregnant."

Emily winced, embarrassed by her illogical accusations. "Yeah, but it didn't matter before we...that is, before we got..."

"Involved?"

"We're not involved. Look, if this declaration is about feeling responsible, then forget it. Nothing has changed. This is my baby. It's no different than if I'd gone to the sperm bank."

"Oh, right. We were just friends, and I was going to be a weekend father. Uncomplicated. But don't you want more than that, Angel?"

"Huh. I'm not the one who insisted we get married."

"Dammit, Angel," Nick shouted. "Listen to what I'm saying. I love you. I've always loved you. And if you weren't so blastedly stubborn, you'd admit you love me, too."

Emily ground her teeth. "I'm not stubborn."

"You're the most stubborn woman in the world. But I'm crazy about you, so I guess I'll have to live with it."

"Gee, thanks. But don't do me any favors."

She heard him growl, and a smile tugged at her

mouth. "What do you think?" Emily whispered down to her round tummy. "Should I believe him?"

The baby stirred, and Emily remembered Nick's wonderment at the life they'd created together.

Okay...so the confirmed bachelor had decided he liked the idea of being a father. That didn't mean he'd discovered eternal love for the mother.

I love you...and if you weren't so blastedly stubborn, you'd admit you love me, too.

She wasn't that stubborn. Determined, of course. But that was a good thing.

"I'm not leaving," Nick warned. "Sooner or later you'll have to let me in."

"You're just confused because of the baby and amnesia and everything." But her voice wasn't as positive as before. "You would have been sentimental about any woman you thought was your wife."

"That isn't true. A part of me did remember...the part that loves you. Angel...if I had all those girlfriends, would I have spent so much time in Crockett? Would you be the first person I call, every time I get home from a job? Would your picture be the only one I've ever carried?"

Emily rubbed her finger across the dead bolt. She wanted to believe him.

"Look at my photo albums. They're all about you. I even have the ribbon I pulled from your hair the day we first met. Remember?"

She remembered. She remembered the fun and laughter and teasing, the years of knowing Nick would always be there, backing her up. It was Nick she'd wanted the night her marriage had finally collapsed. Nick, who knew everything about wanting the baby and helping her have it.

Nick.

Always Nick.

Swallowing, Emily flipped the lock and opened the door. Behind his broad shoulders she saw enough emergency vehicles to film a disaster movie. A loud cheer rose from the crowd when they saw her.

Nick gave her a lopsided smile. "I can't believe you called the cops. What will Mrs. Pickering think?"

"I didn't know you cared."

He looked straight into her eyes, a blend of the gentle, loving man who had first called her his Angel, and the smiling friend she'd always known.

"I care. I'm a little dense, Angel. It's taken me twenty-five years to figure it out, but I love you. I always have."

Emily bit her lip and felt the wall of heartache begin to crumble. She couldn't doubt him. There was too much longing...too much sincerity and need blazing in his face.

"Oh, Nick." Their audience cheered again as she flung herself into his arms. "I love you, too."

Nick held Emily tightly, almost paralyzed with relief. It was all right. She loved him. They'd have a home and babies and everything he'd never dared hope for.

Most of all, he'd have Emily.

He kissed her, whispering the promise of his love into her mouth, again and again.

"I love you, Angel. I'll always love you."

Epilogue

"Angel?"

"Mmm...yes?"

Nick opened the door and smiled at the sight of his wife reclining in the softly bubbling whirlpool. Candles flickered from every available surface, the light gilding her skin and turning her hair into golden fire. She looked drowsy and sexy and utterly enticing.

"Is Katie all right?" she asked.

He closed the door behind him and sat on the edge of the tub. "She's fine. I think she just wanted some attention from her daddy."

"She missed you." Emily reached out and stroked his arm. A lock of hair slipped from the loose knot on top of her head. It dipped into the water and fanned in a delicate veil across her breast. "We both did."

The sultry invitation in her smile was irresistible. Nick started unbuttoning his shirt. "It seemed like forever," he muttered, hardly able to believe that four days could drag out so long. The trip should have lasted a week, but he'd been desperate to get home. By working eighteen-hour days he'd substantially shortened his absence.

He hated to travel alone anymore—nothing seemed interesting or right without Emily—so it was the rare emergency that could drag him away from Washington. Nicholas Carleton, the footloose bachelor, was now firmly rooted in small-town America.

And he loved it.

He adored his two-year-old daughter, so much like her mother with her gold hair and blue eyes. He was crazy about being a daddy and chasing monsters from under the bed and out of the closet. He even liked mowing lawns and cleaning rain gutters. But most of all…he loved Emily. She made everything extraordinary and worthwhile. The loneliness that had once been so much a part of his life was only a memory.

With a wicked smile, he tossed the shirt away and shucked his jeans. "Want to share that bathwater?"

"Are you sure there's room for three?"

Nick froze. *Three?* His gaze swept across Emily's slender body, shimmering with water and candlelight. Yet he also saw the promise of another child, both in her radiant eyes and in a single word.

Three.

"Angel?"

"Yes." She said it simply and sweetly and his chest expanded.

"How far along? Do we have a due date yet?"

Emily laughed, loving the expression on her husband's face. He was like a kid, anticipating a wonderful present. She'd never forget the day Katie was born and the way he'd looked. Proud. Scared. *Ecstatic.*

The quintessential father and husband.

Strong. Loving. Passionate. Still overprotective, but not smothering. He hadn't really changed—he was just more direct in the ways he tried to take care of her.

"I'm only about five weeks along," she explained. She stretched in the tub, arching her back. "Barely pregnant, if there's any such thing."

Nick's eyes glazed.

"No physical changes yet," she said, as though commenting on the weather.

He drew his finger across her breasts, tracing the pebbled outlines of each taut nipple. "I wouldn't say that," he drawled.

Impudently she examined the straining seams of his briefs. "Now *that's* an interesting physical development." She tugged at the navy blue fabric without much success.

With a low, sexy growl Nick slid into the bathwater, briefs and all...it was the *all* that interested Emily. But they both laughed when they realized the water had made the problem worse, and it took a good minute before he could free himself from the confining briefs.

He moved between her legs, less frantic now, their bodies swaying together with the whirlpool jets.

Sometimes their lovemaking was fast and explosive, sometimes slow and sweet and so intense it tore all reason from their minds.

Tonight would be slow and sweet.

A smile curved Emily's mouth. She shouldn't have worried about her ability to respond to Nick. The love

and passion between them didn't owe itself to pregnancy
or amnesia and the shared creation of a baby.

Twenty-five years was an awfully long courtship.

But it had been worth every minute.

* * * * * *

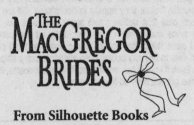
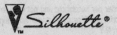

Take 4 bestselling love stories FREE

Plus get a FREE surprise gift!

Special Limited-time Offer

Mail to Silhouette Reader Service™

3010 Walden Avenue
P.O. Box 1867
Buffalo, N.Y. 14240-1867

YES! Please send me 4 free Silhouette Romance™ novels and my free surprise gift. Then send me 6 brand-new novels every month, which I will receive months before they appear in bookstores. Bill me at the low price of $2.67 each plus 25¢ delivery and applicable sales tax, if any.* That's the complete price and a savings of over 10% off the cover prices—quite a bargain! I understand that accepting the books and gift places me under no obligation ever to buy any books. I can always return a shipment and cancel at any time. Even if I never buy another book from Silhouette, the 4 free books and the surprise gift are mine to keep forever.

215 BPA A3UT

Name	(PLEASE PRINT)	
Address	Apt. No.	
City	State	Zip

This offer is limited to one order per household and not valid to present Silhouette Romance™ subscribers. *Terms and prices are subject to change without notice. Sales tax applicable in N.Y.

USROM-696

©1990 Harlequin Enterprises Limited

As seen on TV!
Free Gift Offer

With a Free Gift proof-of-purchase from any Silhouette® book, you can receive a beautiful cubic zirconia pendant.

This gorgeous marquise-shaped stone is a genuine cubic zirconia—accented by an 18" gold tone necklace.

(Approximate retail value $19.95)

Send for yours today...
compliments of ▼ *Silhouette*®
™

To receive your free gift, a cubic zirconia pendant, send us one original proof-of-purchase, photocopies not accepted, from the back of any Silhouette Romance™, Silhouette Desire®, Silhouette Special Edition®, Silhouette Intimate Moments® or Silhouette Yours Truly™ title available at your favorite retail outlet, together with the Free Gift Certificate, plus a check or money order for $1.65 U.S./$2.15 CAN. (do not send cash) to cover postage and handling, payable to Silhouette Free Gift Offer. We will send you the specified gift. Allow 6 to 8 weeks for delivery. Offer good until December 31, 1997, or while quantities last. Offer valid in the U.S. and Canada only.

Free Gift Certificate

Name: _____

Address: _____

City: _____ State/Province: _____ Zip/Postal Code: _____

Mail this certificate, one proof-of-purchase and a check or money order for postage and handling to: SILHOUETTE FREE GIFT OFFER 1997. In the U.S.: 3010 Walden Avenue, P.O. Box 9077, Buffalo NY 14269-9077. In Canada: P.O. Box 613, Fort Erie, Ontario L2Z 5X3.

FREE GIFT OFFER
084-KFD

ONE PROOF-OF-PURCHASE

To collect your fabulous FREE GIFT, a cubic zirconia pendant, you must include this original proof-of-purchase for each gift with the properly completed Free Gift Certificate.

084-KFDR

You've been waiting for him all your life....
Now your Prince has finally arrived!

In fact, *three* handsome princes
are coming your way in

ROYAL WEDDINGS

A delightful new miniseries by **LISA KAYE LAUREL**
about three bachelor princes who find happily-ever-
after with three small-town women!

Coming in September 1997—THE PRINCE'S BRIDE

Crown Prince Erik Anders would do anything for his
country—even plan a pretend marriage to his lovely
castle caretaker. But could he convince the king, and
the rest of the world, that his proposal was real—before
his cool heart melted for his small-town "bride"?

Coming in November 1997—THE PRINCE'S BABY

Irresistible Prince Whit Anders was shocked to
discover that the summer romance he'd had years
ago had resulted in a very royal baby! Now that
pretty Drew Davis's secret was out, could her kiss
turn the sexy prince into a full-time dad?

**Look for prince number three in the exciting
conclusion to ROYAL WEDDINGS,
coming in 1998—only from**

Look us up on-line at: http://www.romance.net   ROYAL

**Beginning in September
from Silhouette Romance...**

a new miniseries by
Carolyn Zane

They're a passel of long, tall, swaggering cowboys who need tamin'...and the love of a good woman. So y'all come visit the brood over at the Brubaker ranch and discover how these rough and rugged brothers got themselves hog-tied and hitched to the marriage wagon.

The fun begins with
MISS PRIM'S UNTAMABLE COWBOY (9/97)

"No little Miss Prim is gonna tame me! I'm not about to settle down!"
—Bru "nobody calls me Conway" Brubaker
"Wanna bet?"
—Penelope Wainwright, a.k.a. Miss Prim

The romance continues in
HIS BROTHER'S INTENDED BRIDE (12/97)

"Never met a woman I couldn't have...then I met my brother's bride-to-be!"
—Buck Brubaker, bachelor with a problem
"Wait till he finds out the wedding was never really on...."
—the not-quite-so-engaged Holly Fergusson

**And look for Mac's story coming in early '98 as
THE BRUBAKER BRIDES series continues, only from**

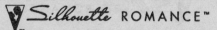

He's able to change a diaper in three seconds flat.
And melt an unsuspecting heart even quicker.
But changing his mind about marriage might take some doing!
He's more than a man...
He's a FABULOUS FATHER!

***

September 1997:

WANTED: ONE SON by Laurie Paige (#1246)

Deputy sheriff Nick Dorelli's heart ached for fatherless Doogie Clay—the boy who should have been *his* son—and the woman who should have been *his* wife. Could they all be blessed with a second chance?

November 1997:

WIFE WITHOUT A PAST by Elizabeth Harbison (#1258)

Drew Bennett had raised his child alone. But then the single dad discovered his former bride Laura was *alive*—but didn't remember their wedded estate! Could he make this wife without a past learn to love again?

January 1998:

THE BILLIONAIRE'S BABY CHASE by Valerie Parv (#1270)

Zoe loved little Genie as her own, so when the little girl's handsome billionaire father appeared out of the blue to claim her, Zoe had only one choice—to marry James Langford in a marriage of convenience.

***

Celebrate fatherhood—and love!—every month.
FABULOUS FATHERS...only in *Silhouette* ROMANCE™

Share in the joy of yuletide romance with brand-new
stories by two of the genre's most beloved writers

DIANA PALMER

and

JOAN JOHNSTON

in

LONE STAR
CHRISTMAS

Diana Palmer and Joan Johnston share their favorite
Christmas anecdotes and personal stories in this
special hardbound edition.

Diana Palmer delivers an irresistible spin-off of her
LONG, TALL TEXANS series and Joan Johnston crafts an
unforgettable new chapter to **HAWK'S WAY** in this wonderful
keepsake edition celebrating the holiday season. So
perfect for gift giving, you'll want one for yourself...and
one to give to a special friend!

Available in November at your favorite retail outlet!

Only from

Silhouette®
™

Look us up on-line at: http://www.romance.net   JJDPXMAS